'Do other men make you react like this?' Julius asked at last, 'or is it only me?'

Jessamy didn't want to answer that question. 'I want a divorce, Julius. This separation has gone on far too long. It's holding both of us back, we're not getting on with our lives in the way we should.'

'I won't agree to a divorce,' Julius warned, and he moved closer, as if trying to intimidate her physically with the powerful bulk of his body.

'You don't have to,' she said defiantly. 'I can get one on the grounds of separation.'

'We're not living apart at the moment,' he reminded her.

'We're certainly not living together!'

'You might have difficulty convincing a judge of that. After all, we've spent the past few days living in the type of place the gutter press likes to describe as a love nest!'

ABOUT THIS MONTH'S AUTHOR

Joanna Mansell writes: 'I don't know if I'm a typical Leo, although I do have a thick mane of hair. But bossy and obstinate? You'd have to ask my family and friends. Or perhaps not—they might say yes! Generous, warm-hearted and creative—that sounds better. I think that, at heart, I'm a rather timid lion, though. I'll have to work at being more like my star sign, and learn how to roar!'

FORGOTTEN FIRE

BY

JOANNA MANSELL

MILLS & BOON LIMITED
ETON HOUSE   18–24 PARADISE ROAD
RICHMOND   SURREY   TW9 1SR

*First published in Great Britain 1992
by Mills & Boon Limited*

© Joanna Mansell 1992

*Australian copyright 1992
Philippine copyright 1992
This edition 1992*

ISBN 0 263 77515 1

STARSIGN ROMANCES is a trademark of Harlequin Enterprises B.V., Fribourg Branch. Mills and Boon is an authorised user.

*Set in 10 on 12 pt Linotron Times
01-9204-53895 Z
Typeset in Great Britain by Centracet, Cambridge
Made and printed in Great Britain*

CHAPTER ONE

JESSAMY woke up on the morning of her twenty-fourth birthday and decided it was time she put her life in order.

It was a decision that she knew she had been putting off for far too long. Next year, though, she would be twenty-five, and that seemed to be some sort of milestone. Before she reached it, she wanted everything that had happened in the past finally to be put behind her.

All the same, just thinking about it made her feel very shaky inside. After all, it wasn't every day that you decided to divorce your husband!

She flicked back the long, dark, silky strands of her hair and sat cross-legged on the bed. Opposite her, piled up on a chair, was a great mound of presents. Last weekend she had gone home to visit her parents, and had come back with a huge bag crammed with brightly wrapped parcels from her mother and father, her three older, married sisters, and all the nieces and nephews they had produced between them. Jessamy had promised faithfully not to open them until the morning of her birthday, and she had kept her promise. She kept all her promises.

Well, almost all of them, she corrected herself, her blue eyes darkening and her mouth setting into an uncharacteristically harsh line. She had broken the very solemn promises she had made on her wedding day, of course. That wasn't her fault, though. *She* hadn't been the one who had walked out.

For just an instant, all the old bitterness began to well up inside her again. Jessamy quickly swallowed it back. It wasn't too difficult. After all, she had had lots of practice over the last four years! And Julius Landor might have ruined a large chunk of her life, but he *wasn't* going to ruin her birthday. He wasn't the only one who could be stubborn and unbending, she decided fiercely.

She pushed all thoughts of Julius out of her head, scrambled out of bed, and began to open her presents. Soon she was surrounded by a mound of gifts, ranging from an expensive sweater from her parents to a small packet of sweets from her youngest nephew. Jessamy treasured them all equally, though. They made her feel loved, and there were times when she needed that very badly.

Next Sunday she was going home for a special birthday tea they were arranging for her. Her sisters, brothers-in-law, nephews, nieces and a couple of aunts were coming over, and it looked like turning into a noisy, boisterous family affair. In the meantime, though, she had to get on with some work. The postman usually delivered bills, not birthday cards!

She ran some bathwater while she sorted her presents into a neat pile. Then she padded back into the bathroom, wriggled out of her nightie, and sank down into the hot water. As she closed her eyes and began to relax, though, she was rather annoyed to find her thoughts drifting back to Julius.

Just because she had decided to divorce him, there was no need to keep thinking about him! Jessamy told herself with a dark frown. Of course, she should have somehow found the nerve to divorce him ages ago. How could she hope to get on with her life while she was still legally tied to him? It made her feel as if he still had some sort of claim over her, and she really hated and resented that.

She decided she would let a lawyer handle absolutely everything. She didn't even want to see Julius again. He could be so overpowering when he wanted to be. And she definitely didn't want to be around when he got the news that she wanted a divorce. She had the feeling that he wasn't going to take it at all well and, like the Taurean bull that he was, he was highly dangerous when aroused. He was quite capable of flattening everything in his path when he gave vent to one of his rare but terrifying fits of temper.

And if he decided that he *didn't* want a divorce? she asked herself with a small shiver.

Jessamy didn't even want to think about that, mainly because she had no idea what she would do then. From bitter experience, she knew it would be impossible to talk it over with Julius, look at the advantages and disadvantages of such a decision, and then reach an amicable agreement. After all, that had been one of the major problems in their marriage. He would never talk about anything, discuss problems or even get involved in arguments with her. He simply made a decision and then stubbornly stuck to it.

She got out of the bath and gave herself a mental shake as she quickly towelled herself dry. Come on, she reminded herself, you're not a naïve little nineteen-year-old any more. You're twenty-four, independent, and with a fairly flourishing career. In fact, you're a girl who's going places—once you've untied yourself from this man who's been like a millstone around your neck for the last four years. And, somehow, you *will* manage to do that.

As she pulled on a pair of faded jeans and a sweatshirt, she made another decision. She was going to contact a lawyer today. In fact, she was going to do it this morning. If she waited for too long, she would simply chicken out. Another four years would drift by, and she would *still* be tied to Julius Landor.

The rattle of the letterbox told her that the postman had just delivered the mail. There were half a dozen cards waiting on the mat, and a couple of letters. Jessamy picked them up, wandered through to the kitchen and put them on the table. She would open them after she had made some coffee.

While the kettle was boiling, she idly glanced at the letters. One looked like a circular, but the other had her name and address neatly typed on the front. She wondered what was in it, and who it was from. The central London postmark didn't give any clues, nor did the good quality envelope. She nearly gave in to the temptation to open it straight away, but the kettle was almost boiling and so she pushed the cards and letters to one side while she spooned coffee and sugar into a mug.

Warm autumn sunshine was streaming in through the kitchen window, and it was very quiet and tranquil. The house was old and situated on the outskirts of London. Jessamy lived in the ground-floor flat, with direct access to the garden through old-fashioned French windows. The two girls who shared the upstairs flat were models, and often travelled abroad on assignments. Both of them were away at the moment, and so it seemed particularly peaceful this morning.

Jessamy sipped her coffee, and at the same time

opened her cards. They were from various aunts and cousins, and she was pleased they had remembered her birthday. Then she picked up the letter with the neatly typed address. Time to find out what was in it, she decided. She had just begun to tear it open when there was a loud, heavy knock at the front door.

She jumped as the sound echoed through the empty house. Who on earth was thumping at the door like that early in the morning? She scowled and almost decided not to open it. It was probably only some over-enthusiastic salesman. Then the knocking began again, even more thunderous this time, and not stopping.

She began to get really angry. Whoever it was, they certainly didn't need to nearly knock the door down! She jumped to her feet and walked quickly through to the hall, her eyes blazing fiercely. When she reached the door, though, she suddenly stopped. She was all alone in the house, and she had no idea who was standing outside. All she could see was a tall, dark shape on the other side of the patterned glass.

Then whoever it was began thumping on the knocker with renewed force, and Jessamy forgot all about being cautious. Instead she wrenched the door open, intending to shout something very rude at whoever had disturbed her quiet, peaceful morning. The angry words dried up in a strangled gasp, though, as she found herself staring into the dark brown eyes of Julius Landor, her husband.

For those first few fraught seconds she just gazed dumbly at him. She couldn't believe he was actually *here*, standing on her doorstep.

Every inch of him seemed nerve-shatteringly familiar, from the dark, dark hair and the rich brown eyes, to the size and shape of him, the texture of his skin, and the arrogant, upright stance of his body. Jessamy found herself staring at the powerful set of his shoulders, and remembered all too clearly that the aura of power wasn't just an illusion. He had a physical strength that more than matched that outward appearance.

She swallowed very hard. Before she could make an effort to get out a few intelligible words, though, he shouldered her roughly aside and strode into the house.

That brought her back to life. This was her home, her sanctuary. No one came here uninvited, and certainly not Julius!

'What do you think you're doing?' she demanded furiously. 'Get out of here. Get out *at once*!'

Julius totally ignored her. Instead he pushed his way into the small lounge and rapidly began sorting through the few books and papers she had left lying on the table.

'Has the postman been yet?' he said in clipped tones.

'I don't see that's any business of yours,' Jessamy shot back. 'Just go away, Julius. I don't want you here. And I don't want you touching anything of mine,' she added fiercely, wrenching out of his hand a book he had just picked up.

He didn't even seem to be listening to her. Instead his gaze swept swiftly round the room. He obviously didn't find what he was looking for, because he pushed her none too gently out of the way, then strode into the small room at the back of the house, where she slept.

Her birthday presents were still piled neatly on the chair in the corner, and her cards stood on the top of the dressing-table. Julius quickly sorted through them, tossing them carelessly on to the floor as he continued his fast but thorough search.

Jessamy stood in the doorway and watched him in angry astonishment. She still couldn't quite believe this was happening. She certainly didn't know *why* it was happening. In the four years they had been separated, she had seen her husband only twice, and both times had been quite by chance. Once had been at the theatre, when she had walked into the foyer and received a thoroughly unpleasant jolt when she had seen him standing only yards away, and the second time had been at a party. On both occasions he had glanced up, as if he had felt her startled gaze resting on him. His eyes had immediately darkened, and his entire body had taken on an aggressive stance. Jessamy's knees had immediately begun to shake, and she had wheeled round and run out.

Afterwards, she had been annoyed by her reaction and ashamed of her cowardice. There was no reason to be frightened of Julius! she told herself over and over again. He had never physically hurt her, although there had been more than one occasion towards the end of their short, fraught marriage when he had looked as if he were making a huge effort to stop himself raising a hand to her.

All the same, it was obviously better if they avoided each other completely. So far they had done precisely that, which made it all the more extraordinary that Julius should be here now, in her flat, actively seeking her out for the first time since he had overridden all his basic instincts and principles and strode out of her life; away from the disastrous shambles of their marriage.

One thing was quite certain, Jessamy thought grimly. He hadn't come here to bring her a birthday present!

But she still didn't have any idea why he had suddenly barged back into her life like this.

She saw him pick up the sweater her parents had bought her for her birthday, then carelessly throw it to one side. That made something inside her snap. She charged into the room and threw herself at him, punching him hard with her small, clenched fists.

'Stop it!' she yelled at him. 'Just *stop it*! Don't you dare touch any more of my things! And if you're not out of here in five seconds flat, I'm going to call the police. You've no right to do any of this—no right even to be here. I don't want you in my home. I don't even want to see you!'

Julius shrugged off her attack easily. He was much taller than her, and those broad shoulders could weather a much harder pounding than she could ever give him. She had forgotten just how strong he was.

He caught hold of her wrists to stop her fists from thumping frustratedly against him.

'Has the postman been yet?' he demanded for the second time.

'I don't see what that's got to do with you being here!'

He shook her fairly violently. 'If you'd just answer my question, I wouldn't have to search all your rooms.'

Jessamy hated being this close to him, hated the iron-hard grip of his hands around her wrists.

'Yes, he's been,' she hissed back at him. She would tell him anything he wanted to know if he would just let go of her, let her get away from him.

Julius didn't release her, though. Instead he pulled her closer and his dark brown eyes bored down into her own fierce blue gaze.

'What did he bring?' When she didn't answer straight

away, he gave her a shake that rattled her teeth. 'What did he bring you, Jessamy?'

For a moment she almost lied to him and told him he had brought her nothing. She had always found it impossible to lie to Julius, though. Something in that dark brown gaze of his seemed to be able to squeeze the truth out of her.

'He brought some birthday cards and a couple of letters,' she spat at him. 'Although I don't know why you're in the least interested.'

'Where are they?' Julius said tightly.

'In the kitchen.'

He released her at once. 'Stay here,' he ordered, and strode out of the room.

There was no way that Jessamy was going to let him walk round her home on his own, though. She was no longer a nervous little nineteen-year-old that he could push around as he pleased.

She rushed after him, almost bumping into him as he came to an abrupt halt in the kitchen doorway. She knew what he was looking at—the pile of birthday cards on the kitchen table, and the letter that she had just started to rip open when he had first thumped on her door.

She heard him take a quick, sharp breath. Then he swung round so that he was facing her.

'Have you read that letter yet?' he demanded.

Jessamy glared at him. 'Is there any reason why I shouldn't have? It is addressed to me! Anyway, why are you suddenly so interested in my mail?'

'*Have* you read it?' Julius said again in a thunderous voice.

Jessamy's legs gently quaked. When Julius lost his temper, it was a fairly awesome sight—and one that she definitely didn't want to witness right at this moment!

'No, I haven't,' she muttered at last.

He picked up the envelope and began to take out the sheet of paper inside.

Her own usually placid temper began to stir. 'That's addressed to me!' she informed him hotly. 'You've no right to look at it!'

Julius took absolutely no notice and continued to remove the sheet of paper. She shot her arm out and tried to grab it from him, but his fingers closed firmly around her wrist and easily held her at bay.

'Give me that letter!' she demanded.

Again Julius ignored her. Jessamy glared at him. Then she swung round and began to walk swiftly towards the door.

'Where are you going?' he asked at once.

'I'm going to find the nearest policeman,' she informed him in an icy voice. 'Then I'm going to bring him straight back here and get him to arrest you. Among other things, I'm going to have you charged with trespassing and interfering with private property.'

'You're not going anywhere,' he told her at once.

'Oh, no?' she retorted. 'Just watch me!'

Before she could make it even halfway out of the door, though, his fingers had gripped hold of her arm again. For a big man, he could move with surprising speed when he wanted to.

'What do you think you're doing?' Jessamy demanded furiously.

'I'll explain later. But for now, you're staying right here.'

'I am not! And if you don't stop manhandling me, I'll——'

She didn't finish her threat, because she didn't actually have any idea what she *could* do. She was alone in the house with Julius, and no one was going to come hurrying to her rescue, no matter how loudly she shouted. It was rather frightening to think how easily men could do what they wanted, simply because of their superior physical strength.

Julius pulled her out of the kitchen, opened the door to the lounge and, with a hefty shove, pushed her inside.

'Stay in there until I tell you to come out,' he instructed.

But Jessamy wasn't going along with that! This was her flat. No one was going to tell her what she could or couldn't do, or where she had to go.

'I've had enough of this!' she informed him hotly. 'You've no right to barge in here or treat me like this. I don't even know why you're doing it, unless you've suddenly gone completely mad. I do know that I'm not going to put up with it for one minute longer, though. I'm going to get a policeman, right now!'

She tried to push past him, to get to the door, but he caught hold of her arm, spun her round and bundled her back into the lounge. Although he hadn't actually handled her particularly roughly, she lost her balance and went sprawling on the floor. He looked down at her, and for a moment looked as if he regretted his actions. Then he glanced at the letter in his hand again, and his face set into a dark, determined expression.

'I haven't gone mad and I'm not in the mood for explanations. And I'm afraid you're going to have to stay in the room for a short time, while I make a couple of phone calls and certain arrangements.'

With that, he slammed the door shut. Jessamy

shakily got to her feet, took a couple of very deep breaths, then stubbornly went over to the door. She *wasn't* going to take orders from Julius. He wasn't a part of her life any more, he had no right to treat her like this!

She seized hold of the door handle and tried to open it. It wouldn't move, though. Julius must have wedged the chair in the hall under the handle, to make sure she couldn't get out.

It was the final straw, being trapped like this in her own flat. For a couple of minutes she gave in to another uncharacteristic fit of temper. She pounded on the door, shouted at the top of her voice, and yelled threats at Julius. None of it brought any response from him. The door stayed jammed shut, and he didn't shout back or answer her in any way.

Very slowly Jessamy began to calm down just a little. She stopped shouting and gave up hammering on the door. Her hands were sore from beating against the hard wood, and she rubbed them absently as she tried to figure out what was going on.

She became aware that her heart was thumping rather hard, although she didn't know if it was from physical exertion, or the shock of suddenly seeing Julius again.

'It's the physical exertion,' she muttered fiercely to herself. 'Julius doesn't affect me in *any way*. All right, so I didn't expect to see him today. In fact, it was just about the very last thing I thought would ever happen. But he definitely doesn't get to me!'

She crept back to the door and pressed her ear against it, trying to figure out what was going on outside. She thought she heard the telephone being used, and the soft murmur of Julius's voice. She couldn't make out what he was saying, though; the door was too thick. Then, a couple of minutes later, it went totally silent, and that unsettled her even further. In fact, the entire situation was completely baffling and highly unnerving.

Was Julius still out there? she wondered. Or had he crept out of the house and left her shut in here? And *why* was she shut in? How long was he going to keep her here?

She ran her fingers through the dark mass of her hair and let out a deep sigh. She certainly hadn't expected anything like this when she had got up this morning. She had thought her birthday was going to be fairly quiet and uneventful. Instead, Julius had erupted back into her life—and only an hour after she had decided to divorce him!

She still had no idea what he was doing here. All she knew was that she wanted him out of her flat—and out of her life—before he managed to do any more harm. It had taken her four years to get over him; four years to get to the point where she could tell herself with some conviction that she had shaken off the last of the memories and was really ready to get on with her life. He *wasn't* going to come charging back, forcing her to remember things she had worked long and hard to forget, turning her entire world upside down for a second time.

They just weren't compatible, she told herself for the umpteenth time. He was earth and she was air. Positive and negative. How could a relationship like that possibly work?

It couldn't—and it hadn't. They had rushed into it too quickly, and lived to bitterly regret their impulsiveness. For Julius, in particular, it had been completely out of character, that headlong dash into such an intense relationship. Jessamy had been swept along by the force of his emotions and, confused by her own emotional and physical needs, hadn't tried to put any curbs on their relationship. Anyway, by then she was sure that Julius would simply have swept any curbs aside.

Until she had met him, she had been a friendly, easygoing girl, with a few not-very-serious relationships behind her, and a very balanced view of life. Julius had changed all that. He had tipped the scales, wrecked the balance. Getting her life back on to an even keel after their break-up had been an incredibly difficult and exhausting battle. There had been times when she had thought she would *never* be able to put herself back together. Even now, she didn't know how she had managed it. She was quite sure, though, that she didn't have the strength to do it all over again.

But she didn't have to, she reminded herself grimly. She was going to divorce Julius, and finally be free of him. He couldn't force himself back into her life. He couldn't get close to her in any way, unless she let him—and she had absolutely no intention of doing that. She might have been soft-hearted and vulnerable once, where he was concerned, but she was a lot older and wiser now. She wasn't risking that kind of insanity a second time.

Jessamy pressed her ear to the door again, then frowned. The flat was still totally silent. What was he doing out there? She scowled. None of it made any sense! She wished she could just go back to bed and start the day all over again, only somehow making it turn out completely normal this time.

A couple of minutes later she heard the chair that

had wedged the door handle shut being moved. Then the door finally opened.

Julius came into the room, and she immediately went over and planted herself in front of him.

'Are you going to tell me what's going on now?' she demanded. 'And, more important, are you going to let me out of here?'

'There's no reason for you to be shut in this room any longer,' he said flatly.

'Good!' she said, and stalked out. She made her way to the kitchen and, to her consternation, Julius followed her.

'I thought you were leaving,' she said pointedly.

'I never said that.'

'Come to think of it, you haven't said very much at all,' Jessamy retorted. 'You just barged in here, grabbed hold of one of my letters, then locked me in my own sitting-room. It's been a really great birthday, Julius. Full of surprises!'

'And that letter would have been the biggest surprise of all, if you'd opened it,' he said grimly.

She stared at him suspiciously. 'Why?'

'Because it was written by someone who seems to have taken a particular dislike to you.'

'What are you talking about?' Her tone was a little more guarded this time.

'I think it could be fairly accurately described as a poison pen letter.'

Her eyes shot wide open. '*What*?'

'It contained vague threats, and called you some rather unpleasant names,' he went on levelly. 'You'd have enjoyed your birthday even less if you'd actually read it.'

'You're making all this up,' she accused. 'No one would want to send me a letter like that!'

'They've already done it,' said Julius, his own eyes giving absolutely nothing away.

'Let me see the letter!'

'No. There's no need for you to read vitriolic rubbish like that.'

Jessamy could see the sheet of paper sticking out of his pocket. She nodded her head slowly, as if she went along with his refusal to let her read it. Then her hand shot out and she whipped the piece of paper out of his pocket, moving so quickly that he had no chance to stop her.

She scuttled over to the far side of the room and had managed to read quite a lot of the letter before Julius came charging after her, taking the paper back from her with such force that it almost ripped in half.

She almost wished he had managed to take it back sooner. Although she had said she wanted to read the letter, the harsh, poisonous words had still sent a huge jolt of shock right through her. Who could hate her so much that they would send her something like that? And the tone of the letter had definitely been very frightening. Threats against her, a suggestion that she should leave the country for a very long time if she didn't want to get badly hurt.

'Are you all right?' asked Julius, looking at her closely.

'Oh, fine,' she said with a loud gulp. 'I mean, letters like that are just a laugh, aren't they?' she rushed on with a very poor effort at bravado. 'You enjoy the joke and then throw them away.'

'I'm not laughing,' he said evenly.

Nor was she. Nothing even remotely like this had

ever happened to her before, and she didn't like it. She didn't like it at all.

With an effort, she started to pull herself together.

'Who sent the letter?' she asked. 'You know, don't you? You must know.'

'I'm—not sure,' he said rather evasively.

'But you must have known that letter was going to arrive this morning, or you wouldn't have been round here, trying to snatch it away before I saw it.'

'I did snatch it away,' he reminded her. His mouth set into a rather grim line. 'I wasn't expecting you to snatch it right back again!'

'You're avoiding the question,' Jessamy said, her voice sharp with nervous reaction. 'How did you know that letter was going to be sent to me?'

'I'd rather not go into that right now. Let's just say that I've got the matter in hand.'

'You've got the matter in hand,' she mimicked. 'Well, I'm afraid that's not good enough for me, Julius. As far as I'm concerned, this is a matter for the police. I'm going to call them, show them the letter, and let *them* sort this out.'

'You might not like the publicity,' he warned her.

'What publicity?' she snapped.

'This is the kind of thing that the press can get very excited about—especially the tabloids. I wouldn't be at all surprised to find them camping on your doorstep, once they get on to this story. I think it would be much better if we handled this ourselves,' he went on smoothly. 'No police and no press.'

'I don't want you to handle anything!' she retorted. 'I can deal with this by myself. Just get out of my house, Julius. I don't want you around. You're not a part of my life any more.'

'That isn't the impression you gave in that newspaper article about you last week.'

Her head came up quickly. 'You saw that article? You read it?'

His face was quite unreadable. 'I skimmed through it. It was a very interesting article. Especially that part where you were described as "the wife of top industrialist Julius Landor." Anyone reading it would assume that we were still living together, and very close.'

Jessamy remembered how very annoyed she had been about that article. The reviewer hadn't even bothered to check on basic personal details. If her marriage had to be mentioned at all—and she didn't see why it was even necessary, it had absolutely *nothing* to do with her work as a book illustrator—then at least they could have got the facts straight, and described her as separated.

She shook her head impatiently. 'We're getting away from the main subject. I want the police to deal with this, and I want you to leave.'

Julius didn't budge an inch. 'I'm not going anywhere,' he told her.

She scowled. 'I don't even know why you're here. If you knew about the letter, you could just have phoned me and told me not to open it. There was no need to barge in, in such a dramatic manner, and snatch it right out of my hand!'

'I simply wanted to make sure you didn't read it. Yes, I suppose I could have phoned, but I didn't even think of that alternative.'

'You obviously weren't thinking straight,' she said a little scornfully. 'That isn't like you, Julius.'

His eyes darkened. 'But I've never been able to think straight where you're concerned,' he said softly.

'I thought you knew that? If I'd been able to think straight five years ago, I'd never have married you. But you've always been able to make me behave completely out of character.'

His words briefly stunned her into silence. It had always been like that. One edged remark, and she would be struck dumb. It was one more reason why she hadn't ever wanted to see him again.

Somehow she found her voice again. 'We both know our marriage was a disastrous mistake,' she said, making an enormous effort to keep her own tone crisp and unemotional. 'And since it's been over and finished with for a long time, there doesn't seem any point in discussing it, especially right now. What I would like, though, is some more information about this letter.'

'And I've told you there isn't any more information I can give you at the moment.'

'I don't believe you!'

Julius shrugged. 'I can't help that. All I can tell you is that someone seems to want to harm you. They obviously hate you a great deal.'

Jessamy gave an involuntary shiver. 'It's frightening to think that sort of person exists.'

His brown eyes became almost black. 'There was a time when you almost hated me that much,' he said flatly.

Before she had time to recover from the shock of that remark, the phone rang, making her jump violently as her raw nerves reacted to the sudden sound. Julius quickly left the room, to answer it. Jessamy knew she should go, it was *her* phone, but somehow she couldn't seem to move.

Julius returned in just a couple of minutes. 'I've made certain arrangements,' he told her. 'That phone call was just to confirm them. Go and pack a few things, enough for a couple of days. You're getting out of here.'

She stared at him blankly. 'What are you talking about?'

Impatience edged his voice. 'I thought it was clear enough. You're leaving this flat.'

'But I can't leave,' she protested. 'This isn't just where I live, it's where I work. And right now I'm in the middle of a set of illustrations for a new book. I've a deadline to meet, I need to get on with my work.'

Exasperation blazed from Julius's eyes. 'Is your damned work more important than your life? Yes, perhaps it is,' he added with deliberate sarcasm. 'There were times when it certainly seemed to be more important than our marriage.'

'*My* work was more important?' Jessamy shot back with furious incredulity. 'You were the one who was the empire-builder! There were days when I never even saw you! I only began to work so hard because it was a way of filling all those empty hours without you.'

Julius seemed about to make an equally impassioned retort, but then stopped. Instead he swung away from her and strode over to the far side of the room.

When he finally spoke, it was in a very different tone of voice—detached, but totally decisive.

'We're getting away from the immediate problem. Until this business of the poison pen letter is solved, you need to get away from this house. It would be dangerous for you to stay here. There's no guarantee that whoever sent it won't follow up those written threats with actual physical violence. Pack some clothes, and whatever you need to finish the illustrations you're working on at the moment, then we'll leave.'

'*We'll* leave?' Jessamy repeated warily. 'I'm not going anywhere with you!'

For just an instant his mouth set into a bitter line. 'Do you consider me more dangerous than whoever sent that letter?'

Jessamy was sure that, in his own way, he was just as dangerous. She would never admit that to him, though. And she had definitely been shaken by the arrival of that letter. She was still trembling a little inside, and the thought of staying here in this house on her own made her nervous. It wouldn't have been so bad if the two girls in the flat upstairs were at home, but they wouldn't be back until the end of the week.

'All right, I'll leave,' she agreed at last in a low voice. 'You can take me to a hotel, somewhere I can stay for a couple of nights until the police can find the very sick person who sent that letter to me.'

'No police,' repeated Julius at once. 'I can deal with this situation.'

Jessamy opened her mouth, ready to start arguing with him, but then closed it. There wasn't any point in going over all that again. Anyway, once she reached a hotel she could simply ring the police from there. Then she could relax and let the professionals deal with this highly unpleasant situation.

In half an hour she was packed. As she picked up her case and walked out of the door, she deliberately didn't look at her husband. She had had enough shocks for one day, and her nerves threatened to become more raw every time she looked into those familiar dark brown eyes.

Jessamy knew that this was the strangest and most disturbing birthday she was ever likely to have

CHAPTER TWO

JESSAMY piled her bags into the boot of Julius's car, then slid into the front seat, which was of soft leather and almost too comfortable.

'Do you know a suitable hotel I can stay at?' she asked.

'I know somewhere that'll be very suitable,' Julius replied briefly.

He switched on the engine, and the car began to move swiftly through the suburbs where she lived.

Jessamy finally began to relax just a fraction. In a short while she would be installed in a quiet hotel room where she could get on with her work, and try to forget about the arrival of that frightening letter.

The car purred onwards, moving easily through the traffic, and eventually a light frown began to settle over her face.

'How much further is it to this hotel? I don't want to stay anywhere too far away from my flat, in case I've forgotten something and need to go back for it.'

'I don't want you to go back to that flat for any reason at all,' Julius instructed her in clipped tones. 'If there's anything you need, then go out and buy it.'

She frowned, but then reluctantly decided that made sense. After all, whoever had sent that letter might even be watching the flat. And if they tried to carry out any of those threats in the letter——

She gave an involuntary shudder. 'Why was that letter sent to *me*?' she said in a small voice. 'I don't have any enemies, I've never hurt anyone. It doesn't make any sense.'

'Perhaps they're using you to try to get to me,' Julius suggested.

Her head came up sharply. 'What do you mean?'

'You might not have any enemies, but I certainly do. Business rivals, employees I've had to fire, people who've got squeezed out in takeover bids——' He gave a small shrug. 'I could probably draw up a long list.'

Jessamy shot him a black look. 'Are you saying it's *your* fault that I've got to leave my home and go into hiding?' Then her brows drew together. 'But we've been separated for four years,' she reminded him in a more reasonable tone. 'Everyone must know that we don't live together, or even see each other.'

'Anyone reading that newspaper article last week might well think we've had some sort of reconciliation, and have got together again,' he pointed out. 'And if they think that, then it makes sense to assume they're trying to get to me by hurting you.'

She looked at him suspiciously. 'You know who's behind this, don't you?' she challenged him. 'You knew that letter had been sent, you even knew it was going to arrive on my birthday. That's why you don't want to go to the police. There's no point, when you already know who wrote it.'

'I'm not absolutely certain and I don't have any concrete proof. That's why I want you to lie low for a couple of days, while I look into it.'

Jessamy muttered something under her breath. She didn't like any of this, not one little bit. It had taken her all this time to put her life back together, and now it looked as if it might be turned completely upside down again, and all because of Julius! He seemed to make a habit of charging through her life and leaving destruction in his wake.

As if he could feel her glowering gaze resting on him, he briefly turned his head and looked back at her. Something inside Jessamy lurched uncomfortably as his dark brown eyes momentarily rested on her. She suddenly knew she had to get out of this car. Spending even this short amount of time with him had been a big mistake. It was already beginning to feel as if the last four years had never happened; as if she were still the confused, angry, raw-nerved girl she had been when he had finally walked out on her.

'I want you to drop me off at the nearest hotel,' she told him in a strained voice.

This time Julius kept his gaze fixed on the road ahead, as if he didn't want her to see his eyes.

'I didn't say I was taking you to a hotel,' he replied evenly.

Jessamy's head whipped round and she stared at him. 'What do you mean?' she demanded edgily. 'Where are you taking me, if not to a hotel?'

'Somewhere I can be sure you won't be in any danger.'

'I'll be safe in a hotel!'

'Possibly,' he agreed. 'But I know somewhere even safer than that.'

The car began to pick up speed, and Jessamy glanced out of the window. She realised that they had just joined the main motorway heading north-west out of London.

'Stop right now!' she ordered.

Julius simply pressed harder on the accelerator and the powerful car responded instantly.

'I want to get out of this car,' she said through gritted

teeth. When he ignored her, the colour flared in her face. 'You can't force me to go anywhere with you. Stop at the next service station, Julius, and let me out.'

Every time she said his name, a funny little quiver came into her voice. And perhaps he had heard it, because he shot a quick glance at her. He didn't say anything, though, and a moment later he returned his full attention to the road ahead.

'You're going to have to stop some time,' Jessamy said furiously. 'Once we leave the motorway, we'll eventually hit a red light or a road junction. Then I'm getting out, and you won't be able to stop me!'

There was still no response from him, and that began to worry her. He seemed to think he could carry her off like this, and get away with it. Well, he would soon find out that he couldn't! she decided fiercely. There had been a time when Julius Landor could reduce her to a whimpering wreck, when his slow-burning but frightening temper roused itself to life. So many times she had felt as if he had just steamrollered his way right over her, refusing to listen to her arguments, just using his overpowering physical and mental strength to get his own way. That was definitely in the past, though. The new Jessamy had learnt how to cope with men, even men like Julius. He was in for a big surprise if he thought he was still dealing with the impressionable, easygoing young girl he had married!

The car continued to purr powerfully along the motorway, effortlessly passing everything in sight.

'If you carry on like this for much longer, you'll soon be stopped for speeding,' Jessamy pointed out, with some satisfaction. 'And you're going to be in a lot of trouble when I tell the police you're keeping me in this car by force.'

'By force?' he repeated, one dark eyebrow delicately lifting. 'So far I haven't laid a finger on you. And I think the police would be fairly sympathetic when I explain that I'm trying to protect my wife from someone who sends sick, threatening letters.'

'Don't call me your wife!' Jessamy said explosively. 'I'm not!'

'Oh, but you are,' he said softly. 'Legally, at least, we're still very much married.'

'I don't care if it's legal or not. I don't feel joined to you in any way.'

'It really doesn't matter how you feel about it,' Julius told her a little grimly. 'The person who sent the poison pen letter certainly thinks of you as my wife. That was what made you a target.'

'You're absolutely certain they're really trying to get at you, aren't you?' she said, with a small frown.

'Yes,' he said, after a moment's hesitation.

'What did you do, to make them hate you so much?'

'I don't know. I don't deliberately turn people against me. I just get on with my work and my life.'

'No, you don't,' Jessamy said a little wearily. 'You barge through life, Julius, knocking people aside as you go. And the worst of it is that you don't even *see* those people you knock over as you charge along.'

'In business, it simply isn't possible to be polite and considerate all the time,' he said tersely. 'You have to be as single-minded and relentless as your rivals if you want to get to the top.'

'And that's where you always wanted to be, wasn't it?' she said with a slow shake of her head. 'Right at the very top of the heap. And now you're finally there. Are you enjoying your success, Julius? Was it worth all the hours and hours of work, the sacrifices, the lack of room in your life for anything—or anyone—else?'

'It wasn't like that,' he said with unexpected tightness.

'Wasn't it?' Jessamy gave an uncharacteristically cynical smile. 'Well, it's funny, but that's exactly how it seemed to me.'

'Once I began to put together my chain of companies, I had certain responsibilities to the people I employed,' Julius said in the same curt tone. 'And I was taught from an early age that you don't turn your back on those kind of responsibilities.'

'It's a pity you weren't also taught a little kindness and tolerance. Taught how to be a nicer human being!'

'So now you're criticising not just me, but my parents,' he said, his eyes darkening.

'Oh, yes, your parents,' Jessamy said with a distinct grimace. She remembered Julius's parents very well indeed. *Too* well, in fact. They were like two permanent scars on her memory.

His father, the Colonel, with his ramrod-straight back, still using his title even though he had retired from the Army more than twenty years ago. Jessamy also remembered his clipped, completely unemotional voice, mainly because she had occasionally heard an unnerving echo of it in Julius's own voice, when he was deliberately being distant.

And then there had been Julius's mother, always dressed in dark, expensive suits, with every strand of her silver hair set firmly into place. Jessamy had known straight away that nothing would ever throw her off balance, that she would deal with life's disasters and crises in a calm, dispassionate way, finally resolving them to her own satisfaction.

Of course, Jessamy's arrival on the scene as Julius's fiancée had obviously been a major crisis. Naturally, nothing had been openly said. In fact, his parents had both been excruciatingly polite to her, but that had only made it even more obvious that she wasn't the kind of wife they wanted for their clever, ambitious son.

'It's so important that Julius's wife is socially acceptable,' his mother had murmured to Jessamy while they had strolled around the gardens, ostensibly admiring the immaculate flower beds. 'You must let me introduce you to some of the people we know. And, of course, if you ever need any help organising dinner parties or entertaining any of Julius's important business clients, I'd be delighted to give you some advice. Julius needs to maintain a certain lifestyle, and you might find it difficult at first to cope with the demands he'll make on you.'

By that time it had been made very clear to Jessamy—in the politest way possible—that she definitely *wasn't* socially acceptable. In fact, she wasn't acceptable in any way at all. They clearly considered it would be disastrous for Julius to marry a girl nearly twelve years younger than he was. A girl who wore her long dark hair loose, who practically lived in jeans and sweatshirts, and who always seemed to have a couple of paint stains on her somewhere because she was trying to scrape a living by producing exquisitely detailed illustrations for books.

His parents had been right, she thought with a small sigh. It had been a mismatch right from the very start. It was just that she had been too much in love at the time to see it. Air and earth, she told herself again, her brows drawing together in a grimace. She should have known she would end up getting trampled by Julius, the Taurean bull.

'You never liked my parents, did you?' said Julius in an angry tone, breaking into her memories.

'It wasn't a question of not liking them. We just couldn't communicate in any way. I often felt as if we came from different planets!'

'They never tried to dissaude me from marrying you.'

'Because they were clever enough to know that they couldn't,' Jessamy said a trifle bitterly. 'Anyway, they knew they didn't *have* to dissaude you. All they had to do was sit back and wait for it all to fall apart. And they didn't have to wait long, did they? I bet even they were surprised at how little time it took!'

'I think that surprised everyone—including me,' Julius said grimly.

His breathing had become rather quick and heavy, and the car suddenly swerved a few feet, as if he was no longer paying any attention to the road ahead. A nearby car blared its horn loudly and, to Jessamy's intense relief, Julius seemed to get control over himself again very rapidly, steering them back on to a straight course.

'Why don't you stop, before you cause an accident?' she demanded.

'I'll stop when we get to where we're going,' he said shortly.

'And where's that?'

He didn't answer. Jessamy hadn't really expected he would.

A few miles further on they left the motorway, although they were still following a main road. The signposts told her they were heading towards Oxford.

Good, she thought with some relief. Oxford was always crowded. The traffic would force him to slow down, and probably stop altogether at some point. Then she could jump out and make a run for it.

She had no clear idea where she would go, and what she was going to do in a strange city with no money. That didn't seem important. Getting away from Julius was the top priority. All the other problems could be sorted out when that had been accomplished.

To her disappointment, though, they didn't go through Oxford but skirted round it. The traffic kept flowing steadily, giving her no chance to escape. Shortly afterwards they turned off again, on to a more minor road. That eventually took them down the wide, steep main street of a small town, then the road narrowed, crossed an old stone bridge, and began to climb, leaving behind the houses, the church with its tall, graceful steeple, and the half-timbered buildings. Jessamy realised they were leaving Oxfordshire and entering the Cotswolds, with their rolling uplands and wooded valleys, tiny villages with golden-stoned houses, and swift-flowing rivers.

Why had they come here? she wondered uneasily. As far as she knew, Julius had never liked the countryside. In the early days of their marriage they had lived in the very heart of London, close to the centres of business, art and culture. At the time she had supposed it had been a reaction to his upbringing, all those years spent in his parents' elegant Georgian house on the edge of a quiet, beautiful Sussex village. She had thought he had had enough of all that rural tranquillity, and had wanted to live somewhere lively and sophisticated. Had she been wrong about that? she now wondered. Perhaps they had only lived in London because he had thought it was what *she* wanted. It was just one more thing they had never actually talked about.

The road they were following was almost empty. It was mid-autumn, and the bulk of the tourists who thronged through the picturesque villages in the summer had gone. The weather was still warm and sunny, though, an Indian summer that looked like stretching on for a few more days yet. Yet, despite the brightness, Jessamy suddenly felt cold. Something was happening here, something she didn't understand. And she didn't think that it was totally connected with the arrival of that poison pen letter this morning.

As unease spread through her again, she swung round to stare at him. 'Where *are* you taking me?' she demanded, wishing there was some way she could force an answer out of him.

'You'll find out in just a few minutes,' Julius replied. 'We're almost there.'

The narrow road they were following was overhung with oak and chestnut trees, their interlaced branches letting through thin, bright shafts of light that flickered and danced over the car as it passed underneath. Then Julius reduced speed as they approached another small village. Houses lined the road, built of the local Cotswold limestone that weathered to different shades of gold that glowed in the warm sunlight. Late roses tumbled over stone walls, Michaelmas daisies and chrysanthemums provided bright patches of colour, and the trees that surrounded the village were beginning to show the first hint of the glowing autumn colours still to come.

Then the village was left behind and the road began to wind gently upwards, through more trees, towards the head of the valley. Before it reached it, though, the road suddenly dipped down again and ran into a shallow hollow filled with sunshine. And set in the centre of the hollow was a house that was a picturesque jumble of gables and tall chimneys, uneven roofs and latticed windows.

A narrow drive ran through a garden that was full of late summer flowers that were still blooming in the warmth of the autumn sun, and large, spreading trees that threw irregular patches of shade. Low stone walls divided the garden up into different segments, and these were marbled with moss and lichen in a dozen shades of gold and green, and often hidden completely under tumbling masses of roses, clematis and ivy.

The car finally came to a halt outside the house, and Jessamy looked around, a small frown drawing her brows together.

'It's beautiful,' she conceded at last. 'But why have we come *here*?'

'Because this is where you're going to stay. It's the one place I can be sure you'll be perfectly safe.'

'But I can't possibly stay here,' Jessamy said promptly. 'It's too far away from everything.'

'What exactly do you mean by "everything"?'

'Well—London, my flat, libraries where I can get reference books, *civilisation*,' she finished with a touch of exasperation.

'We're only thirty miles from Oxford, and less than twenty miles from Stratford-upon-Avon. And I think they're both regarded as fairly civilised,' Julius remarked.

'You know what I mean,' she snapped, glaring at him. 'Anyway, I don't want to stay here!'

'What you want is rather irrelevant in this particular

situation. You'll be well away from any danger here, and that's the only thing of any importance.'

'I don't have to stay in the middle of nowhere to be out of danger,' she retorted. 'I'd have been perfectly safe in a hotel.'

'Don't you like it here?'

'It's lovely—if you like this kind of thing. But I'm a city girl, I was born in London and I've lived there all my life. It's too quiet in the countryside, nothing ever happens. You know what I'm talking about, because you're exactly the same. You like the noise and the bustle of the city, you wouldn't want to be stuck out here, with nothing but trees and flowers to look at, and no one to talk to but the birds or a passing rabbit!'

Julius looked at her. 'Do you really think you know what I want? What I like?'

'Well—yes,' she said, only a little more uncertainly this time. 'Anyway, who owns this place?' she went on, trying to cover up the fact that she had been thrown rather off balance by that last challenge. 'A friend of yours? Well, tell him it's kind of him to agree to let me stay here, but I'm turning down his invitation.'

'I own this place,' Julius told her evenly. 'And I live here.'

Jessamy blinked hard, sure she must have misheard him. His voice had been clear enough, though.

'But—you can't live here,' she said at last.

'Why not?'

'Because——' She floundered a little and then tried again. 'Because it's not your kind of place. You grew up in the countryside and you couldn't wait to get away from it! When we were married, you bought a flat right in the very centre of London.'

'When we were first married, I knew you would have

to spend quite a lot of time on your own, when I was tied up with business affairs. I decided it would be better for you if we lived in London because there would be places you could go, friends you could visit. And I knew you liked city life, and wouldn't be happy in the country.'

Jessamy blinked. 'You mean we lived in London because you thought it was what *I* wanted?'

'Didn't you?'

'Well—yes,' she admitted. 'But I didn't know—I didn't realise—I mean, I thought you wanted it too. You never said you didn't.' And now they were back to one of their major problems, she thought a little grimly. All those times when Julius had refused to talk about anything of any importance. She decided she didn't want to think about it. She looked round, and changed the subject. 'How can you run a business empire from a place like this?'

'I can be in London in under a couple of hours,' Julius replied. 'And my business interests are spread throughout the country, they're not confined to the capital. Living here isn't a problem.'

'Well, it would definitely be a problem for me!' she retorted. 'Please take me straight back to London.'

Julius didn't even bother to reply. Instead, he got out of the car and slid the keys into his pocket, making it very clear that he didn't intend to take her anywhere.

For a few seconds Jessamy sat there quietly fuming. Then she scrambled out of the car, slamming the door shut behind her.

'You're not going to take me, are you?' she challenged him. 'Well, that's fine by me. I've got legs, I can walk!'

'It's going to take you a very long time,' said Julius in an unruffled voice. 'London's rather a long way.'

'I've got credit cards,' she shot back defiantly. 'I'll buy a train or coach ticket.'

The only trouble was, her account was rather overdrawn at the moment. She didn't think her bank manager would be very pleased if she ran over her credit card limit as well. She certainly wasn't going to admit to Julius that her finances had got into a bit of a mess, though.

'In fact, I can probably hitch-hike,' she added. 'I don't think I'd have too much trouble getting a lift.'

Julius's eyes darkened a couple of shades. 'Don't you think that would be rather dangerous?'

'I'm getting used to living dangerously,' she retorted. 'And after being sent a poison pen letter and then meeting you again, hitching a lift seems pretty tame stuff!' She walked round to the back of the car. 'Please unlock the boot, so I can get my bag out.'

To her surprise, he took the keys from his pocket and unlocked the boot. He lifted her bag out but, instead of handing it to her, he kept a firm grip on it and began to walk towards the house.

'Where are you taking that bag?' she yelled at him.

'The same place as you're going,' he replied, his voice still remarkably calm. 'Into the house.'

'How many times do I have to tell you I'm not setting foot inside that house?'

He gave a brief, unconcerned shrug. 'As many times as you like, but it won't change anything. You're staying here.'

'You can't make me!'

At that, Julius turned back to face her, and she saw that his features were a lot less calm than his voice. A dangerous light glinted in his eyes, small lines flared around the corners of his mouth, and his colour was slightly heightened.

'Oh, but I can,' he said softly.

'Because we're still technically married?' Jessamy threw at him scornfully. 'Do you think that gives you some kind of hold over me? Well, you're very wrong about that! I'm a free and independent person. You can't force me to do anything.'

Julius put down her bags and slowly walked back towards her. As he drew nearer, Jessamy felt a distinct tremor run right through her nervous system. He could be so very intimidating when he put his mind to it—and he definitely looked in the mood to be *extremely* intimidating right now!

All the same, she stood her ground, and refused to let any of her sudden nervousness show on her face.

He finally stopped when he was just a couple of feet away from her. As far as Jessamy was concerned, that was much too close. There wasn't anything she could do about it, though, except back away, and she certainly wasn't going to do that! If she did, he would know at once that there were certain ways in which he could still get to her. That kind of knowledge could be highly dangerous, and she would do just about anything to keep it from him.

Instead, she flicked back her long dark hair and stared defiantly at him.

'Are you going to hand over that bag and let me leave here?' she demanded.

'If that's what you want,' Julius replied, to her surprise.

Suspicion instantly rushed through her. Julius never gave in easily, not over anything.

'What's the catch?' she asked warily.

'No catch. Just take your bag and walk out of here.'

But Jessamy didn't move. She knew her husband too well. She had heard him use that tone of voice in the past and knew exactly what it meant.

'All right,' she said slowly, 'let's suppose I walk out of here. What happens then?'

'There are a couple of possibilities. You could be very stupid and go straight back to your flat, in which case you could be putting yourself in a lot of danger. Then, of course, there'll be all the publicity to cope with, once the press get hold of this story.'

'Why should the press want to cover that kind of story?' she challenged him. 'I'm no one important, they're not interested in me.'

'But they are interested in me,' Julius reminded her. 'And not just in my business life. They'd love to have the chance to pry into my personal affairs.'

Jessamy knew he was right about that. She had seen photographs of him in the papers, sometimes on his own, but more often escorting a beautiful woman to various functions. She had never wanted to look at those photos for too long. Even after four years, they could make every nerve in her body sing with pure jealousy.

She gulped hard. 'They won't know anything about your personal affairs—unless you tell them.'

'That's right,' he agreed, looking directly at her. 'And if you leave here, I'm afraid I'm going to have to make a few phone calls. I'll put the press on to you so fast they'll be camping on your doorstep before you're even halfway home!'

She stared at him in disbelief. 'You wouldn't do that!'

His dark brown eyes met hers, and she flinched at the ruthlessness that blazed from them. 'Try me,' he invited softly.

Jessamy tried to swallow, but couldn't, her mouth and throat were bone-dry.

'You're just bluffing,' she said, her teeth openly chattering despite the heat of the afternoon.

'I never bluff. Not in business, or in my private affairs. I intend to keep you here, Jessamy, and I don't much care what I have to do to accomplish that.'

'But why?' she burst out.

'I told you, you'll be safe here. And your safety's important to me.'

'I don't see why. Nothing else about me seems to have been very important for the past four years!'

Julius was silent for a while. Then he said in a calmer voice, 'Well, perhaps I'm just trying to make up for lost time.' He looked at her levelly. 'What's your decision, Jessamy? Are you going to stay here for a couple of days, where you'll be safe? Or go back to your flat and have to cope with more poison pen letters—and the press?'

'I don't think I'll be particularly safe here,' she muttered.

'Because of me?' he asked, an odd light briefly shining in his eyes.

'No, not because of you!' she shot back at once. 'You're no threat to me, because you don't mean anything to me any more.' She ignored the dark anger that suddenly showed on his face, and went on, 'If this is your house, then whoever sent that poison pen letter must know about it. They'll just start sending them here, instead of to my flat.'

'Hardly anyone knows about this place,' Julius

replied. 'I've a flat in London that I use when I'm in town, and I always give that as my home address. Only a handful of people know I own this house, and none of them would reveal that information to anyone.'

Jessamy found herself rather intrigued by his admission. 'You mean, it's your personal hiding place? A sort of retreat from the world? I wouldn't have thought you needed somewhere like that.'

'There's a great deal that you don't know about me.' Then, as if he regretted saying that, he abruptly swung away from her. 'Let's go into the house.'

'I haven't yet said that I'm staying here,' she said stubbornly.

'You don't actually have any choice, do you?' he said, in a very cool voice.

He was right, of course. She didn't. Perhaps that was the most disturbing thing about this whole affair, the fact that he had so easily taken away her freedom of choice. And on the very day when she had woken up and decided to divorce him, to celebrate the fact that she finally had a life of her own; a life which didn't include Julius Landor. Under different circumstances, she might have been able to appreciate the irony of it.

Her legs felt absolutely leaden as she trudged after him towards the house. Four years apart, and yet he was still able to manipulate her. It was hard to believe that this was actually happening; harder still to accept that she couldn't do anything about it.

As they approached the house, she looked up at it without much interest. It was clearly old, and several additions had obviously been made over the years, although they all blended together easily and harmoniously. Julius unlocked the heavy, carved front door, and went inside.

Jessamy followed more slowly, and found herself walking through a large hall in what was probably the oldest part of the house. The floor was stone-flagged, there was an enormous fireplace on the far side, and the windows looked out on to the gardens. It was fairly sparsely furnished, with a long oak trestle table, a few hard-backed chairs, and a large sideboard. The furniture was clearly old, and had been chosen with some care to fit in with the atmosphere of the hall. Although the wood was dark, to match the panelling and the massive smoke-stained beams that supported the high ceiling, there was nothing in the least depressing about the room. The sunlight that filtered through the windows mellowed the old wood and brought out the richness of its colour, and even the stone floor glowed softly and didn't give any impression of coldness.

Jessamy refused to admit that she was impressed in any way, though. 'Not exactly homely,' she muttered.

'I don't live in this part of the house,' said Julius. 'I'm still renovating and furnishing much of it. The place was almost derelict when I bought it.'

He led her through an archway at the far end of the hall. 'This is the wing I'm using at the moment,' he told her. He pushed open the door nearest to him. 'This is the drawing-room.' She had a quick glimpse of another sun-filled room, but one that was much more comfortably furnished, with a sofa and armchairs, bookcases, small tables, and television, video and stereo equipment. Then Julius closed the door again and started up the winding staircase nearby. 'The kitchen's at the back of the house, but you can see that later. I'll take you up to your room first.'

When they reached the first floor, he opened one of the doors and she walked into a large bedroom with a huge bed, masses of cupboard space, a comfortable armchair, and a table and chairs set by the window.

'If you don't like this room, there are several more you can choose from,' Julius told her.

'I suppose this room is as good as any other,' she said with a deliberate lack of enthusiasm. Then her dark brows drew together. 'Where do you sleep?' she asked guardedly.

'At the far end of the corridor. Although I can move to another wing of the house, if that makes you feel happier.'

'Nothing about this situation makes me feel in the least happy,' she shot back at him. 'And I suppose it doesn't really matter where you sleep. Although I'd actually prefer it if you moved back to your flat in London while I'm staying here. That way, I wouldn't have to see you or speak to you at all!'

Her rudeness had some effect, she noted with satisfaction. Colour showed along his cheekbones, and his mouth set into a very taut line. With some effort, though, he refrained from retaliating.

'We're both staying here, so you might as well get used to that idea.' He tossed her bags into the room. 'I'll leave you to settle in and unpack. Come down when you're ready, and I'll show you the rest of the house.'

'I'm not interested in a guided tour,' she told him coldly. 'I'm not a tourist. In fact, as far as I can see, I'm a prisoner!'

'Don't twist things too much, Jessamy,' he warned her. 'I've a limited amount of patience—as I'm sure you'll remember.'

There were a lot of things that she was beginning to remember about Julius—but she wanted to forget them again as quickly as possible! It was *dangerous* to remember things about Julius.

'Just go away,' she muttered. And to her intense relief, he went, closing the door behind him with unnecessary force.

Jessamy ignored her bags, leaving them standing by the door. Instead, she went over to the window and stared out at the bright flowers, the trees, the green of the grass and the hills that rose up gently all around the house. The sun shone down on her through the glass, and added to the headache that was gathering behind her eyes.

This was the very last place on earth she wanted to be. She didn't like the countryside, and she didn't like Julius Landor. She had to get away from here!

The only trouble was, she just couldn't see how she was going to manage it.

CHAPTER THREE

JESSAMY stood at the window for a very long time. In the end, though, she turned tiredly away and began unpacking her bags.

She hated doing it. It was like an admission of defeat. Right now, though, she couldn't see any alternative. She found it hard to believe that Julius would actually carry out his threat to tell the press about that letter, but she couldn't be absolutely *sure* he wouldn't do it. It was four years since they had parted, and who knew how much he had changed during that time? It was a chance she simply couldn't take. Jessamy prized her privacy far too much, she couldn't bear to have a pack of journalists prying into every corner of her life.

When she had finally finished unpacking, she went and sat by the window again. She didn't want to go back downstairs and have to see Julius, speak to Julius. And the worst part was that she didn't know how long she was going to have to stay here. Julius had said he would deal with this situation, but who knew how long it could take? And what if he never discovered for certain who had sent that letter? What on earth would she do then?

Jessamy gave a small shiver and decided she didn't even want to consider that possibility. Think positive! she advised herself. That's the only way you're going to survive this.

In the end, she got very bored with staring out of the window at all the greenery outside. The birds were singing, the sun was shining, but Jessamy wasn't in the mood to appreciate any of it. She gave a dark scowl, left the room and trudged downstairs, her mood so prickly that she knew it would only need one wrong word from Julius to trigger off her own temper. She wasn't usually like this, she usually had a fairly relaxed attitude towards life. Only Julius could make her behave like this.

When she got downstairs she headed towards the back of the house, with the vague idea of finding the kitchen and making herself a drink. The house seemed to be an absolute maze of rooms, though, and it was several minutes before she finally opened a door that led into a surprisingly well-equipped kitchen.

Her mood didn't improve when she saw that Julius had got there before her.

'I'm just checking on dinner,' he said, as she stalked in. 'It's almost ready.'

'Dinner?' she repeated, her eyebrows shooting up. 'I didn't know you'd taken up cookery! And what exactly are we going to eat?' she went on sarcastically. 'Something you threw together while I was unpacking?'

'It's a casserole,' Julius replied equably. 'And I could have thrown it together—I'm not completely incapable of producing a simple meal—but on this occasion, I didn't. Mrs Copely from the village acts as my housekeeper whenever I need her. She keeps the place clean and dusted, and prepares the odd meal for me, if I'm too busy to do it myself. I rang her from your flat just before we left, and told her that we'd be arriving later. I also asked her if she could leave a meal in the oven.' His dark brown eyes glittered briefly. 'I didn't think you'd be volunteering to cook dinner after you arrived here.'

'You're certainly right about that,' Jessamy retorted. 'I don't mind getting my own meals while I'm here, but I'm not the dutiful little housewife any more, Julius.'

'You were never that,' he said more softly. Before she could say anything, he added, 'And I didn't want you to be.'

'Didn't you? Then what *did* you want me to be? You certainly didn't seem to like me the way I was!'

Jessamy found she was breathing rather heavily, and she could feel her skin growing hot with colour. Stop it, stop it! she instructed herself through gritted teeth. Don't mention the past, don't get drawn into any more arguments about it, don't even *think* about it, or things are just going to fall apart.

Julius seemed a lot less equable than he had been earlier. He prowled over to the far side of the kitchen, then slammed down a couple of plates, as if he were suddenly finding it very hard to control his own temper.

'I didn't bring you here to open up all the old wounds again,' he growled at last.

'Of course not,' she shot back sarcastically. 'You brought me here so that I'd be safe. Only I never feel safe when I'm around you. I think I'd sooner face whoever sent that poison pen letter!'

With that, she whirled round and hurried out of the door that led into the garden. She found herself standing on a wide terrace, with steps that led away from the house. Afraid Julius might be coming after her, she ran down the steps and into the garden, following the paths that led between wide beds of herbaceous flowers, many of them still blooming happily in the warmth of the long, sunny autumn.

She finally came to a halt at the very far end of the garden. For a few moments she thought she was

trapped, with no way through the high walls that
surrounded this part of the garden. Then she saw a
wrought-iron gate set in the corner, and hurried
towards it. Right now, she felt desperately in need of
an escape route.

To her relief, it wasn't padlocked. It swung open on
well-oiled hinges, and she found herself in a much
wilder part of the garden, with tall grass, spreading
trees, and a large pond fringed with rushes.

She began to walk forward rapidly, but a couple of
minutes later she came to an abrupt stop. Where was
she going? If she kept on walking, then she was simply
going to get lost. Nothing lay ahead of her except the
thickening belts of trees that ringed the head of the
valley.

There was also something else to consider. If she ran
away from Julius every time the conversation touched
on the past or got in the least personal, then he was
going to start to think he could still get to her. She
didn't want that to happen. She didn't dare *let* it
happen. It would put her in a position where she was
totally vulnerable, and vulnerability was something
Julius was very good at exploiting.

She stood there for a long time, thinking the whole
thing out. Finally she turned round and, slowly and
very reluctantly, began to make her way back towards
the house.

When she went through the door that led back into
the kitchen, she found that Julius was still there. He
was sitting at the table and staring ahead of him with a
dark, brooding expression.

For a few moments he didn't seem to realise she was
there. Jessamy looked at him and found herself noticing the changes in him. His hair was still thick and

dark, but it was a little longer. When she had first known him, the glossy curls had been ruthlessly cut into a very short, severe style that would have suited very few men, but looked exactly right with his strong features. His mouth was exactly as she remembered it, with the well-defined lips, just full enough to give an unexpectedly sensual outline. The small lines at the corners were new, though, and they were echoed in the faint lines of tension etched around his eyes. They were the same, of course, that rich shade of brown that lightened and darkened as his mood changed. It had never been easy to guess what he was thinking and feeling from looking at his eyes, but it was almost impossible now. They were carefully guarded, as if they hid secrets he didn't intend ever to reveal to anyone. And his face itself had taken on an almost gaunt look, the strong bone-structure rigidly marked, and the skin itself only lightly tanned, despite the hot summer they had just enjoyed.

Then Julius glanced up at her, and for just an instant Jessamy seemed to see right through the protective shield with which he had surrounded himself. She was hit by a wave of familiarity; the sudden realisation that *this* was the man with whom she had shared so much, if only for a very short time. Love, a surprising amount of laughter, physical pleasure that had left her literally gasping for breath at its intensity——

As if abruptly realising that she was seeing too much, Julius's eyes went blank again, deliberately shutting her out. Jessamy wanted to shout at him in sheer frustration. How many times in the past had he done that to her? He had always seemed grimly determined never to let her close to him, except physically, and in bed he had wanted her almost too much. He had

sometimes half frightened her with his need for her. At
other times—especially in the beginning—he had succeeded in arousing a desire in her that matched his
own, and that had been almost as frightening. She had
somehow always thought that love should be made
with the mind as well as the body. With Julius, though,
it had always been so very physical, and she hadn't
been able to stop herself from responding to that great
flood of passion.

She had the feeling that Julius, too, was having some
trouble controlling his memories of the past. He took a
rather deep breath, got to his feet, and didn't sound
quite like himself when he finally spoke.

'Life isn't going to be very pleasant over the next
couple of days if we can't spend any time together
without arguing.'

'I don't expect it to be pleasant,' Jessamy retorted.
'I didn't want to come here, and I certainly don't want
to stay here. Why don't you let me go now, before the
situation gets even worse?'

'You're going to remain here,' he said with absolute
finality.

She scowled at him. 'You're so stubborn!'

'I'm also still your husband. And as far as I'm
concerned, that makes me responsible for your safety.'

'And that's what I really hate about all this,' she shot
back at him fiercely. 'I'm not *me* any more. I'm your
wife, I'm a responsibility, I'm someone who has to be
dumped somewhere safe, like a child who can't look
after herself. Well, I'm none of those things! If you
weren't blackmailing me with that threat to set the
press on me, then I'd be out of that door in half a
second flat!'

For just an instant Julius's own eyes flickered into

life. Jessamy took an involuntary step backwards, because something about his expression definitely alarmed her. A little too late, she remembered that it wasn't a good idea to goad Julius's temper into life. Then, to her relief, his face set into controlled lines and the dangerous light in his eyes dulled again.

'If you'd behave sensibly for once in your life, then I wouldn't have to make any threats at all,' he said in a rather grim tone. 'But since we're both going to have to stay under this roof for a couple of days, perhaps even longer, maybe we'd better lay down some ground rules so that we can at least avoid open warfare.'

'That's fine by me,' Jessamy replied at once. 'As long as you remember that I want to see you as little as possible. And you'd also better take into account the fact that I want to get on with some work while I'm here. I don't intend to sit around all day doing nothing.'

A dark look crossed his features as she told him she didn't want to see him, but he still kept his temper on a tight rein. 'If you want to work while you're here, that's fine by me. What do you need?'

'A room with lots of good natural light, and a large table where I can spread out my things. I also need privacy,' she added rather pointedly. 'No interruptions.'

'In other words,' said Julius in a tight voice, 'although this is my house, you don't want me to set foot in that room.'

'Exactly. In fact, come to think of it, there's no reason why we should see each other at all. This house is more than large enough for us to live quite separately.'

He shot a black look at her. 'What are you suggesting? That we divide the house into two, and each of us keep to our own half?'

'Well, I suppose that isn't very practical,' she conceded. 'And as you said, this *is* your house. I suppose that gives you some rights.'

'Thank you,' he said with uncharacteristic sarcasm.

'Just give me a room to work in, and the rest of the time I'll keep out of your way as much as I possibly can. I suppose I'll have to use the kitchen,' she added, thinking out loud now, 'but we could work out some kind of rota. That way, we won't have to bump into each other every mealtime.'

'And what if we should accidentally meet?' Julius enquired, a dangerous glint beginning to show in his eyes. 'Do we pretend we haven't seen each other? Or apologise, and scuttle out of each other's way?'

'Of course not,' she said a little impatiently. 'We'll have to see each other occasionally. But we can simply say "hello", and leave it at that.'

'Are you sure you can manage that much conversation?'

Jessamy didn't like the continuing note of sarcasm in his voice. It was unlike him. She remembered him as being arrogant, overbearing, impatient, irritable and downright angry, but never sarcastic.

'All I'm trying to do is to find a solution to the problems we're bound to run into if we're living under the same roof,' she said stiffly. 'But if you're not willing even to try and be helpful——'

Julius suddenly looked unexpectedly weary. 'All right,' he said, getting to his feet, 'I'll be as damned helpful as you like. I'll give you a room to work in, I'll turn round and walk the other way whenever I see you, and I'll stay out of the kitchen whenever you want to use it. Do you want this arrangement to start right now? Shall I take my meal somewhere else to eat it?'

Jessamy immediately stared at him suspiciously. It wasn't at all like Julius to give in so easily. On the other hand, perhaps he was simply agreeing to her demands in order to avoid another argument. It had been a long and exhausting day, and she had to admit that she felt as tired as he looked.

Funnily enough, though, and despite everything she had just said, she didn't want to eat dinner on her own. She knew it didn't make any sense, not after she had spent most of the day wishing she were a thousand miles away from Julius, but she suddenly felt rather desperately in need of human company—even Julius's. She supposed the tensions and upsets of the day were finally getting to her. And if she sat all alone in this unfamiliar kitchen, the silence of this big old house would definitely start to unnerve her.

'I suppose we can both eat here, in the kitchen,' she muttered. 'Just for tonight,' she added quickly, so he wouldn't think she was about to change her mind about anything else.

'Just for tonight,' he agreed flatly.

He dished up the casserole, and they ate in silence. The food was very good, but Jessamy ate mechanically and didn't really taste it. And Julius ate hardly anything at all. His dark brown gaze kept fixing on her, though, which eventually ruined what little appetite she had left.

'Why do you keep staring at me?' she demanded edgily at last.

'Am I?' He seemed genuinely surprised. 'It wasn't intentional.'

After that, he didn't look at her at all. For some

reason she found that just as unnerving. As soon as she had forced down the last of her food, she pushed her plate away and stood up.

'I'm going up to my room. Unless you want me to help with the washing-up?'

'There's no need for that. I'll put everything in the dishwasher.'

She walked over to the door, but then stopped and looked back at him. There was one more question she couldn't stop herself asking.

'Julius, do you really like living here? This is the last place on earth I'd expect you to set up home.'

'It isn't a home,' he said. 'Not yet.' His gaze fixed on hers and held it unblinkingly. 'I was brought up in the countryside. When I bought my first company and began to build up the business, I had to live in the city, so that I was at the centre of things. But I've found that a few years away from something can make you realise just how much you want it—need it.'

Something in those dark brown eyes set every one of her nerves on edge. And what did he mean by that last sentence?

Nothing! she told herself very firmly. But he was looking at her with a dark intensity that made her nerves quiver very oddly. She wanted to run out of the room, to get away from that intent gaze, but stopped herself. She had run away from him once already today. She wasn't going to do it again, and let him think that she could still be affected by anything he said, or by the way he looked at her.

With a huge effort she forced herself to walk away slowly, almost nonchalantly. It wasn't until she was completely out of his sight that she allowed herself to break into a swift trot. And when she was back in her bedroom, she was relieved to find there was a bolt on the door. Without any hesitation, she shot it into place. Then, at last feeling fairly safe, she allowed herself to sink into the nearest chair, totally drained by everything that had happened since she had woken up this morning.

She stayed in the chair as dusk crept over the garden below, too physically and mentally tired to move. When full darkness had finally fallen, she dragged herself to her feet, wriggled out of her clothes and crawled under the shower.

She was relieved that her room had its own bathroom. At least she wouldn't run the risk of bumping into Julius in the shower. That would have been highly embarrassing—and a lot of other things she didn't even want to think about.

Jessamy slowly dried herself, pulled on a nightdress and flopped into bed. Despite her tiredness, though, she couldn't sleep. The thought of Julius being so close—just a few rooms away—was more than enough to keep her awake.

She had never expected to be this close to him again. She certainly hadn't expected to find herself sharing a house with him! And she didn't understand what was going on inside his head, which she found disturbing. Of course, she had *never* known what Julius truly felt. He could be amiable, even friendly on the surface, while underneath a lot of suppressed strong emotions were churning away. But this time, that situation seemed even more dangerous than usual. If only he would talk to her. . .

Jessamy gave a small sigh. It was no use wishing for the impossible. She closed her eyes again, tossed and turned for a long time, then finally managed to get a couple of hours of disturbed sleep.

When she woke up again, just after daybreak, for a few moments she couldn't remember where she was. Her gaze slid round the unfamiliar room, then she suddenly gave a loud groan as everything slid back into place. She was in Julius's house, in the middle of the Cotswolds.

She knew she would feel slightly better about the situation if he were forcing her to stay at his flat in London. At least she could step out of the door and be among people; she would hear the familiar sound of traffic whizzing past the door at all hours of the day and night. Here, there was nothing to disturb the silence but birdsong. Although it was barely daylight, they were already twittering and tweeting away at full pelt. Even that was better than the silence that surrounded the house at night, though. All the time she had lain awake, it had been so quiet it had quite unnerved her.

The sun crept up into the sky, with the long chain of warm, golden days remaining unbroken. Jessamy eventually hauled herself out of bed and padded over to the window.

She had to admit that the view wasn't at all bad. The colours of the flowers glowed brightly in the early morning light, the grass was covered with a light beading of dew which made it gleam, and the leaves of the trees hung in perfect stillness, with not even a breath of breeze to ruffle them.

Jessamy quickly dressed, then left the bedroom. The house was as silent as the garden outside. She wasn't used to that either. Usually there was the sound of music drifting down from the flat above, the knock of the postman, and the chink of bottles as the milkman delivered the morning milk.

She made her way to the kitchen and was relieved to find it empty. A quick hunt through the cupboards and the fridge revealed a good supply of food, but for the moment she only wanted coffee.

She was just boiling some water when the door opened and Julius walked in. His eyes flickered momentarily, then he retreated behind a withdrawn expression which gave absolutely nothing away.

'I didn't think you'd be up this early,' he said.

'It must have been the noise that woke me up,' Jessamy retorted sarcastically.

Julius almost smiled. 'The silence does take some getting used to,' he agreed. 'But after a couple of days you won't even notice it.'

'After a couple of days I hope I'll be able to go home!' she shot back at once.

Any suggestion of a smile that had hovered around his mouth instantly disappeared.

'It may take longer than that to find out who sent you that letter,' he said rather shortly.

Jessamy stared at him suspiciously. He wouldn't keep her here any longer than was absolutely necessary, would he? No, of course he wouldn't, she tried to convince herself. Why would he do something like that? He couldn't *like* living with her under these sort of conditions.

'I suppose you want some coffee?' she muttered edgily.

'Yes,' he said. Then his gaze met hers challengingly. 'That is, if you don't mind being in the same room as me for a few minutes?'

'I know I said last night that there was no need for

us to spend too much time together, but I didn't mean we should take it to extremes,' she said with some annoyance. 'All the same, it makes sense to come to some kind of agreement about this. For a start, we could work out some kind of rota for using the kitchen. We'll begin with today. Would you rather take an early or late lunch?'

Julius's mouth suddenly set into a hard line that she remembered very well, and her nerves gave an involuntary quiver.

'This is absolutely ridiculous,' he said in a terse voice. 'Can't we even eat a meal together occasionally? We're meant to be two mature, civilised adults, so why can't we behave like it?'

'Because I don't feel mature *or* civilised when I'm anywhere near you,' Jessamy threw back at him fiercely. 'And no, I don't like feeling like that, which is why I'm trying to avoid you as much as possible!'

She glared at him, her blue eyes overbright. At the same time, she knew it had been a big mistake to lose her temper like that. It gave too much away. She had been quite unable to stop herself, though.

Julius's gaze raked over her sharply, then settled on her face. She had the feeling that those dark brown eyes were noting every little detail, from the bright flush of her skin to the faint quiver of her lower lip.

'At least you're not indifferent to me,' he said at last, in a very different tone of voice. 'After all this time, I wondered if you might be.'

'I don't see that it matters what I feel or don't feel, where you're concerned,' she retorted. 'It's all irrelevant now. We're separated in every sense of the word.'

Despite her defiant words, though, she had the feeling that she had made a bad mistake during these last few minutes. Every time she shouted at him or reacted to something he had said, it seemed to reveal something she had never meant to let him see.

Angrily she turned her back on him. She wished he would walk out and leave her on her own. She didn't want to look at him or talk to him again today.

Julius obviously wasn't going anywhere, though, at least not yet.

'Do other men make you react like this?' he asked at last. 'Or is it only me?'

Jessamy opened her mouth, but then snapped it shut again. She didn't want to answer that question.

'When I first met you you never lost your temper,' he commented softly. 'You were always relaxed and easygoing. It was one of the things I liked about you.'

'People change,' she said curtly. 'And if you don't like me the way I am now, then that's very easily remedied. Let me leave here.'

Julius's face set back into implacable lines. 'You're not going anywhere.'

'Don't you trust me?' she challenged him angrily. 'Do you think I'm going to do something stupid, like going back to my own flat? Or ignoring the fact that the sender of that poison pen letter might try to do me some very real harm?'

'I trust you, and I don't think you'll do anything stupid,' he said, to her surprise. 'But you're staying here,' he added, in a very final tone of voice.

'*Why?*' she demanded stormily.

'I don't want to go into my reasons right now.'

'You never want to go into your reasons for doing *anything*,' Jessamy threw back at him. 'Trying to talk to you is like trying to charge through a brick wall. All that happens is that you keep bouncing off it, and in the end you just get hurt!'

'Is it really as bad as that?'

Something in his voice made her look up at him. For just an instant she seemed to see right into his eyes, past the protective barrier that he instinctively put up against intruders. Jessamy wished again that she knew what was really going on inside his head. Something was brewing there; something she was sure she wasn't going to like. This wasn't just about poison pen letters, and bringing her here for her own safety. Something else was going on, she was sure of it. What, though? Oh, if only he would just tell her what he was thinking, what he was feeling, what his plans were.

She gave a frustrated shake of her head. It would be a lot easier to wish for the moon!

'I'm tired of arguing,' she muttered at last. 'It isn't getting us anywhere. I want to get on with some work. What room can I use?'

'There's a large drawing-room at the back of the house that should be suitable.' His own voice was calmer now, as if he were relieved at being back on safer ground. 'It's quiet and the light's good, so I think it'll be ideal. If it isn't, there are plenty of other rooms to choose from. Just look around until you find one that's suitable.'

'And what are *you* going to do all day?'

'I'll find a way of passing the time.'

Jessamy looked at him rather warily. She didn't like the idea of him prowling around inside the house while she was working. 'Shouldn't you be working as well?' she suggested. 'All those companies you own can't run themselves. I shouldn't think you could afford to take a couple of days off at such short notice. I mean, there

must be meetings you have to go to, people you've got
to see, things that have to be organised.'

'Having to take an unscheduled break is certainly
inconvenient,' Julius agreed. 'But I don't think any of
my companies are going to collapse simply because I'm
not around for a short time. If they do, then I've been
running them very inefficiently and incompetently. But
you're right, there are several things that have to be
dealt with immediately. That's why I telephoned
Eleanor last night and asked her to come to the house
this morning. She's bringing some files I have to work
on. And while she's here, I'll give her the instructions
she'll need to keep things running smoothly while I'm
away.'

Jessamy's face, which had begun to clear, instantly
darkened again.

'Oh, yes,' she muttered, 'the elegant Eleanor. I
should have known that she'd still be with you.'

Eleanor was Julius's secretary. She was almost the
same age as Julius, and had been with him for over ten
years.

A different expression crossed Julius's own face.
'She was someone else you never liked, wasn't she?'

'What do you mean, someone else?'

'Eleanor, my parents, quite a few of my friends—
you never really made any effort to get along with the
people who'd been an important part of my life before
you came on the scene.'

'And how many of them made any effort to get along
with me?' she exploded.

'They tried very hard to accept you.'

'None of them tried very hard at all!' Jessamy
retorted furiously. 'But you wouldn't know that,

because most of the time you weren't even there. Eleanor saw far more of you than I did!'

'We worked together,' Julius said tautly. 'Of course we saw a great deal of each other.'

'Do you know she would never let me speak to you on the phone? Every time I rang up, she was ready with some excuse. You were out of the office, you were at a meeting, you were with an important client and couldn't possibly be disturbed.'

'All those things were very probably true,' Julius said, his voice quite cold now.

'Every single time?' she demanded.

'I was expanding my business interests and working almost every hour of the day. It was totally demanding, I never seemed to have a free minute. But you were too young to realise just how much work you have to put in at that stage of building up a business, how much effort it takes to hold the whole thing together and stop it from collapsing around you.'

'And Eleanor understood that?' Jessamy said scornfully.

He paused for a few moments. 'Yes, she did,' he said at last.

'While I was too young to understand any of it. Too young for you even to try and explain what you were doing, how important it was and how much it took out of you. But not too young for you to marry!'

Julius's dark brown eyes glittered brightly. 'At that stage in my life I never intended to marry anyone. But there you were, so beautiful, so untouched. I knew I shouldn't rush into it, all my instincts told me to take it slowly. But, in the end, I couldn't resist you.'

'What a shame for us both that you didn't have more willpower,' Jessamy said bitterly. 'But let's get back to

Eleanor, since she's going to be arriving here shortly. Has she changed over the years? Is she still as loyal? Still in love with you?'

'Stop it, Jessamy!'

But she couldn't stop. 'Did you use her as a consolation after we split up? More fool you if you didn't. She's always wanted you, always hated me.'

She had gone too far. She knew it, but couldn't turn back; couldn't wipe out any of the things she had already said.

'Are you jealous of Eleanor?' Julius asked abruptly.

'When we were married, I was jealous. You spent so much time with her, I felt she even knew you better than I did. But don't make the mistake of thinking I'm still jealous,' she added fiercely. 'As far as I'm concerned, she can have you. You don't belong to me any more. In fact, I don't think there was a time when you ever *did* belong to me.'

'Not even when we were lying so close that every inch of our skin touched from head to toe?' he challenged her softly.

Jessamy was immediately horrified by the vivid pictures and memories that his murmured words conjured up inside her head.

'You've probably lain like that with dozens of women,' she threw back at him, not caring what she said as long as she could exorcise the intimate pictures still flashing through her mind.

'Even if I had, do you think it would have been the same with them as it was with you?'

She glanced a little desperately towards the door. She had to get out of here!

'I've no idea if it would have been the same or not,' she said rather wildly. 'When we were married, I never

...eping with other women. I suppose I ...and naïve to realise that you must have ...active sex life before you met me. And now ...on't care. *I don't care*,' she repeated with fresh ...emence.

'Are you sure of that?' His eyes were fixed on her with such intensity that she felt as if that dark brown gaze were burning her skin.

'Oh, yes, I'm sure! I've spent four years making very certain I don't care. I never want to go through anything even remotely resembling our marriage ever again. I'd rather stay single and celibate for the rest of my life!'

Julius started to say something, but Jessamy didn't want to listen to any more. She wrenched open the door behind her, ran through it, slammed it shut behind her, then dashed out of the house.

CHAPTER FOUR

JESSAMY was halfway down the drive when she saw the car approaching. It came to a halt just a couple of yards away, and her stomach gave an uncomfortable lurch as the door opened and Eleanor got out.

It had been four years since Jessamy had seen her, and she didn't seem to have changed at all. She was still tall and slim, her gold hair was styled into soft waves that perfectly framed her face, and her clothes were immaculate. Since she was the same age as Julius, she had to be in her mid-thirties, but her skin was smooth and unlined. She was the sort of woman that most men would look at at least twice and, unless totally senile, would find extremely desirable.

'The elegant Eleanor', Jessamy had nicknamed her, all those years ago. That description fitted her perfectly. Every inch of her was glossy and sophisticated.

Today, though, she looked much more ruffled than usual. In fact, a rather strange expression crossed her face when she saw Jessamy standing there, as if she wasn't in the least pleased to see her.

Since, at that particular moment, Eleanor was the very last person that Jessamy wanted to see, the feeling was mutual. Her heart was still thumping after that disturbing scene with Julius, her skin was hot and clammy, and her eyes overbright. As well as that, compared with the elegant Eleanor, Jessamy felt downright scruffy. As usual, she was wearing faded jeans, a baggy T-shirt, and her long dark hair tumbled down her back. She felt comfortable in casual clothes and wore them most of the time, but she found herself wishing that, just for once, she had put on something rather more dressy.

As Eleanor walked slowly towards her, the expression on her face didn't change. 'Hello, Jessamy,' she said, as she drew nearer. Her voice was like the rest of her, cool and classy. 'I thought you'd be at the flat in London. I didn't expect to find you here at Julius's country retreat.'

'I didn't expect to be here,' Jessamy said, rather shortly.

Eleanor gave a small frown. 'When Julius phoned me yesterday and asked me to bring the files he wanted to work on, he didn't tell me you were staying here.'

'Well, you know Julius,' said Jessamy, with a small shrug. 'He never gives out details of his personal life.' Then she looked rather curiously at Eleanor. 'Why did you think I'd be at Julius's London flat?'

'Oh—there have been rumours going around that the two of you had got together again.'

It was very obvious from Eleanor's tone of voice that she didn't like this new development in the fractured relationship between Julius and his wife. Jessamy didn't really care, though. Whatever happened between her and Julius was none of Eleanor's business. Yet she found that she *did* care that Eleanor had used Julius's Christian name so freely. She supposed she was perfectly entitled to do that, since she had been his secretary for more than ten years, but for some odd reason it had still made her nerve-ends prickle antagonistically when Eleanor had said his name.

Eleanor's gaze had returned to her now. Then it began to sweep slowly over her in the deprecating manner that Jessamy remembered so clearly from four years ago. Finally she lifted her head and gave a confident smile. It was clear that she still didn't consider Jessamy was capable of holding Julius's interest for very long. Why would a man like him be attracted to a girl who, for a lot of the time, looked rather like a gypsy? those cool green eyes seemed to say. He might find her a novelty for a while, but novelties soon wore off.

On the other hand, Jessamy derived some satisfaction from the knowledge that Eleanor didn't seem to have got one iota further in her own subtle pursuit of Julius.

The sound of footsteps on the gravel behind them put an end to the confrontation between the two women.

'Hello, Eleanor,' Julius said shortly, as he strode up to them. 'Thank you for coming. Did you bring the files I asked for?'

'All the files and outstanding correspondence are in the car,' she replied.

'Good.' He glanced at Jessamy, then let his gaze return to Eleanor. 'I see that you've met my wife.'

'Yes,' said Eleanor. It was such a short word, and yet she managed to put an amazing amount of meaning into it.

'Are you ready to get on with some work, then?' Julius said rather curtly.

'Of course. You know that I want to do anything I can to help.'

If she really wanted to help, she could leave! Jessamy thought balefully. This situation was difficult enough without Eleanor barging in and making it even worse.

She was already taking the files out of the car,

though, gracefully leaning over and showing long, well-shaped legs.

'We'll be working in the usual room,' Julius told her, in the same curt tone. 'Go straight up there and I'll be along in a couple of minutes.'

As soon as she had disappeared through the front doorway, Jessamy swung round to face Julius. 'So, you're going to be working in your usual room? Eleanor obviously comes here often!'

'She's only been here a couple of times, when I needed to work on some papers very urgently.'

'For someone who's only been here twice, she seems very familiar with the layout of the house,' Jessamy retorted. 'And I noticed she's brought a lot of work with her. I wouldn't be at all surprised if it were too much to get finished in one day—which would mean that she'd have to stay overnight.'

'That's a possibility,' Julius replied coolly.

'And is that a regular arrangement?'

'Would it bother you if it were?'

His eyes had suddenly fixed on her keenly, as if he were finding her reaction very interesting. Far too late, Jessamy realised that she had tumbled straight into a trap. She shouldn't be showing any interest at all in the relationship between Julius and his secretary.

'Of course it wouldn't bother me!' she replied at once, but she had the awful feeling that her denial lacked the ring of truth.

Julius's mouth twisted into a disturbing smile. 'No, of course not,' he agreed. His eyes were gleaming, though, as if he had found the conversation very enlightening.

To Jessamy's intense relief, he didn't say anything more. Instead, he turned round and strolled back to the house, leaving her standing there with a black scowl on her face. Why did she keep reacting like this, and saying the wrong thing? He was beginning to get entirely the wrong impression, and that really annoyed—and disturbed—her.

She waited until Julius was out of sight, then slowly walked back to the house herself. She would get on with some work, she told herself firmly. That would take her mind off of everything—including Julius, and the fact that he was going to spend the day working closely with Eleanor.

Not that she cared that they were going to be spending so much time together, she reminded herself hastily. It didn't matter to her in the least. It was just that she disliked Julius's secretary so very much. And it was definitely a mutual antipathy.

When Jessamy reached the house she collected her painting materials, rough sketches and a couple of books she thought she might need, then made her way to the drawing-room where she was going to work. She set everything out on the table, then stared at the blank sheet of paper in front of her and gave a small sigh.

Inspiration seemed to be at a very low ebb. She was meant to be illustrating a new book for children, a fantasy story by a well-known author. The illustrations had to be of ruined castles and dark forests, mythical monsters and fire-breathing dragons, unicorns, trolls and goblins, and a golden-haired boy who fought against the forces of the night. And they all had to be executed in the delicate, exquisite detail that had become Jessamy's trademark.

She sighed again and sorted through the rough sketches. None of them was quite right yet. And the deadline for submitting the illustrations was getting uncomfortably close.

She doodled a small, ugly dwarf, then a couple of unicorns. Finally she tried to get down to some more serious work, first skimming through a book about castles she had brought with her, then sketching ruined towers, broken archways and towering keeps.

They looked fine, but they didn't have any atmosphere. Jessamy pushed them irritably to one side and began to work on one of the dragons, filling in some of the more intricate details. That went quite well, and she was fairly pleased with it. She took a quick break for lunch, gulping down a couple of sandwiches and a cup of coffee, then spent the afternoon painting the dragon, using dozens of different shades so that he shimmered with colour.

By the end of the day she was tired but satisfied. Perhaps working in a place like this wasn't such a bad idea after all. It was certainly a lot more quiet and peaceful than her flat in London. And the trees that surrounded the house sometimes had a slightly spooky look, in the half-light of the late evening. Maybe she could use that in a couple of her illustrations.

She carefully cleaned her brushes and put away the paints, then realised she was very hungry. Apart from those couple of sandwiches, she hadn't had anything to eat all day.

She trotted along to the kitchen, but when she reached it, she stopped and listened carefully before opening the door. She didn't want to go waltzing in if Julius and Eleanor were already there, enjoying a quiet meal together! To her relief, though, the kitchen was empty. She went in, hunted through the cupboards until she found everything she needed, then cooked herself a large meal.

By the time she had eaten it and cleared away the dishes, dusk was beginning to fall. This might be a good time to spend half an hour in the gardens, sketching shadowy clumps of trees and bushes, she decided. She went back to the drawing-room to collect a sketch-pad and an assortment of pencils. Then she wandered out into the grounds.

The sun had dipped below the horizon, leaving only a soft golden glow in the air. Jessamy walked through the wilder part of the garden and then sat on a fallen tree-trunk, rapidly sketching the shadow-filled path that led round to the pond, the twisted shapes of the tree boughs, and the dark clumps of rushes. Then an owl suddenly hooted nearby, making her jump, and she hastily decided she had done enough for one evening. This place was *very* spooky once the bright sunlight had disappeared. She didn't want to be here when it was completely dark.

Instead of returning through the back entrance of the house, though, she strolled round to the front. The air was soft and unseasonally warm, and she was reluctant to go back indoors. That move turned out to be a mistake, though. As she approached the front entrance, the door suddenly opened and Eleanor came out.

Jessamy immediately wrinkled her nose. It looked as if the serenity of the evening had just come to an end!

Eleanor began to walk towards her car, which was parked on the drive just a few yards from where Jessamy was standing. Then she saw Jessamy, and her cool green eyes became positively frosty. She didn't say a word to her, but instead opened the boot of the car and loaded in the folders she had been carrying.

'Have you finished all that work you brought with you?' Jessamy asked with some interest, moving closer.

'Yes,' Eleanor replied shortly.

'You must have worked very hard.'

'Julius worked almost non-stop.'

'How very disappointing for you,' Jessamy said sympathetically. 'You must have thought you'd brought enough work to last at least a couple of days. And now you're not even going to get the chance to stay overnight.'

Eleanor's lovely mouth set into a not particularly lovely line. 'Do you think I'm disappointed at not spending more time with Julius?' she said bluntly. 'I'm not. I see him almost every day. We spend more time together than many married couples.'

Jessamy's own expression changed at the direct challenge. 'It doesn't seem to make any difference how much time you spend with him,' she said equally bluntly. 'You've been with Julius for ten years now, and you're still just his secretary.'

Eleanor's lips suddenly relaxed into a secretive smile. 'Am I?' she said.

Jessamy's stomach gave an uncomfortable lurch. She's bluffing, she told herself uneasily.

'Why did you come back?' went on Eleanor, her green gaze bright with dislike as it fixed on Jessamy. 'You're no good for Julius. You never were.'

'How do you know that?' Jessamy said defensively.

'Just take a look at yourself.' The older woman's tone was completely dismissive now, and contempt showed clearly on her face as her eyes raked over Jessamy's paint-stained T-shirt and faded jeans. 'You don't even know how to dress. Do you really think the wife of a man like Julius should slop around all the time in old jeans and dirty sweatshirts?'

'My clothes aren't dirty,' Jessamy retorted in an angry voice. 'They're just paint-stained. And I dress to suit the kind of life I lead. It hardly makes sense to wear elegant suits and designer dresses when I'm painting!'

She was immediately annoyed with herself for becoming defensive. What business was it of this woman how she dressed?

'You never fitted in with Julius's lifestyle,' Eleanor went on relentlessly. 'You never even tried. He couldn't take home business associates for dinner because he was embarrassed for them to see you. Anyway, you couldn't have coped with a sophisticated dinner party. You'd have probably served them a frozen TV meal! And you hounded him at work, wanting his attention all the time like a spoilt child. You weren't mature enough to realise that running a large and expanding business concern requires a huge amount of concentrated hard work.'

Jessamy had gone quite white while Eleanor was saying all of those things. For a few moments she felt nineteen again, unsure and nervous, easily browbeaten because she had very little self-confidence.

Then the feeling passed, and she was the new Jessamy again. The Jessamy who knew her own worth; who knew she was going to lead her own life, instead of always trying to do what others wanted and expected of her.

'How dare you say all those things to me?' she snapped with sudden fierceness. 'You know *nothing* of what Julius really wants from his wife. And perhaps our marriage didn't last long, but I had more of him than you'll ever have. And that's what you really can't stand, isn't it? You think you're better than I am in just about every way, more beautiful, more clever, more experienced. But Julius didn't want perfection. He wanted a home, someone he could love, someone he could relax with. He wanted *me*. And let me tell you something else, Eleanor. You've been with Julius for ten years now, and if a man hasn't wanted something in ten years, then he's never going to want it. I might have lost him, but you've never even had him. And you're never going to!'

The older woman's face had set into a white mask. Jessamy knew she had been cruel, and a part of her was already regretting it. Yet it had been Eleanor who had started this war of words; Eleanor who had tried to interfere in something that should have been none of her business.

The older woman opened the car door, then turned round to shoot one last ashen-faced look in Jessamy's direction.

'Do you think you can get him back?' she said tightly. 'Is that why you're here? Well, you can't. You don't get a second chance where someone like Julius is concerned. And even if a miracle somehow happened and he agreed to try again, it would simply end up exactly the same way it did the first time. You'd just go through the whole disastrous fiasco all over again, because not one thing about you has changed.'

'You're wrong about that, Eleanor,' Jessamy said steadily. 'I might look the same on the outside, but inside me there's a very different person. And you've made a mistake about something else. I don't *want* Julius back. None of that will make any difference to you, though. Whether I'm here or not, Julius is never going to turn to you. You should do what I've done, cut yourself completely free of him and make a new life for yourself.'

Eleanor ignored that last piece of advice. 'If you've made a new life for yourself, what are you doing here?' she challenged.

'Believe it or not, I'm not here by choice.'

'I certainly don't believe you. And if I possibly can, I'm going to stop you wrecking Julius's life a second time.'

Jessamy suddenly ran out of patience. 'Don't you think *my* life was wrecked as well?' she shouted at her. 'I've spent the last four years trying to pick up the pieces!'

'Whatever happened to you, you deserved it,' Eleanor said icily. 'And I hope you stay unhappy for the rest of your life.'

With that, she got into the car, expertly revved up the engine and swiftly drove off.

Jessamy stood in the centre of the drive, beginning to shake a little with reaction. Why had she ever got involved in that slanging match in the first place? she wondered with a dark surge of anger.

Still deeply disturbed by what had happened, she didn't hear the sound of approaching footsteps behind her.

'Has Eleanor gone?' asked Julius's voice a few moments later.

The sound of his voice made her visibly jump. 'Yes— yes, she has,' she said edgily. 'Why? Was there something you wanted to tell her before she left?'

'Nothing that can't wait. I can ring her at the office

tomorrow.' His eyes narrowed slightly. 'What were the two of you talking about?'

'Nothing very important,' Jessamy answered evasively.

One of his dark eyebrows slid upwards. 'No? From a distance, it looked like a rather interesting conversation.'

Jessamy abruptly shook her head. 'No, it wasn't interesting! It was——'

'What was it, Jessamy?' he asked, and his dark brown eyes bored into hers, as if demanding an answer.

But she ignored his last question. 'Why did you bring her here?' she muttered instead. 'You know we don't get on.'

'I thought you might have outgrown all that old animosity.' His voice took on a thoughtful note. 'It's interesting that you haven't.'

'You don't get over disliking someone simply because you haven't seen them for a long time.' Jessamy gave a small scowl. 'Is she coming here again?'

'That rather depends on the pressure of work,' Julius replied non-committally. 'Would you prefer it if she didn't?'

'This is your house,' she pointed out frostily. 'You can bring whomever you like here.'

'But you didn't like seeing her here, did you? And you certainly don't want her to come here again.' His eyes fixed on hers. 'Perhaps you'd prefer it if I went even further, and fired her?' he suggested softly.

'You wouldn't do that,' she said at once.

'Wouldn't I?'

'Of course not,' Jessamy said at once. 'After all, she's the perfect secretary, isn't she? Anyway, where would she go if you fired her? That job is her entire life. What would she do?'

'There are a dozen equally good jobs she could walk into.'

'This conversation isn't going anywhere,' she said with sudden impatience. 'You're *not* going to fire Eleanor, and especially not if I ask you to.'

'Why not try me?' he invited.

His dark brown gaze locked on to her own wide open blue eyes, and it took an enormous effort for her to look away from him.

'I think you're playing games with me,' she said rather angrily. 'And I don't like it. I want you to stop!'

His eyes began to darken. 'What if I can't?'

'Don't do this, Julius,' she warned, beginning to back away from him. 'Remember, I know how you operate. You like to confuse people, and then you suddenly charge at them and trample them underfoot while they're caught up in that confusion. Well, I've been trampled too often, and it isn't going to happen again. Those tactics won't work with me any more, I know you too well.'

'You don't know me at all.'

His flat statement seemed to hang in the air between them. Then Jessamy responded angrily.

'You never *let* me know you!' They stood there for a few more seconds, staring at each other. Then Jessamy made a desperate attempt to put an end to this before the tension between them reached an even more dangerous level. 'And I don't want to know you!' she threw back at him. 'Just remember that and we might— just might—be able to get through the next few days without any major problems.'

She turned and ran back to the house before he

could say anything else. Julius stood and watched her go, and wondered what else she would have said to him if she had known the complete truth; that he had known from the very start exactly who had sent that poison pen letter to her. That, quite by chance, he had seen a copy of it on Eleanor's word-processor.

His secretary had been out to lunch, and he had been going through the files stored on the disk she was currently using, looking for a copy of a contract that he urgently needed to check. Instead he had found the poison pen letter that she intended to send to Jessamy. There was even a second letter—more vitriolic than the first—and the date she meant to send it.

Julius couldn't remember when he had last been hit by such a wave of anger. But when he had fought back the overwhelming urge to ring the police and have criminal charges brought against his secretary, he had realised he could use this to his advantage. Could use Eleanor in order to get close to Jessamy.

Julius Landor was a stubborn man. That stubbornness had got him through the last four years, but he had finally had to admit that walking out on his wife had been the biggest mistake of his life. Now he was determined to put that mistake right. Eleanor had given him the opportunity he had needed. For now, he would use her. But when this was over, Eleanor would deeply regret that she had tried to interfere with his personal life.

He turned round and walked off into the gathering darkness. He knew now what he wanted. But he wondered if Jessamy would ever forgive him when she found out what he had done in order to try and achieve it.

*   *   *

Jessamy had run back into the house. Her legs were shaking, and she couldn't forget about that confrontation with Julius. Suddenly, even the sound of his voice seemed to be getting to her. The whole thing was beginning to frighten her very badly, because her peace of mind depended on her staying indifferent to Julius. If she couldn't do that, then she was in very serious trouble.

She made very sure that she stayed well out of Julius's way for the rest of that evening. Another restless night followed, and she determinedly settled down to work again the next morning, concentrating hard on the illustrations so that not even a tiny corner of her mind was free to think about Julius.

By the end of the day she was beginning to feel slightly more relaxed. The illustrations were going unexpectedly well and the emotional ups and downs of yesterday were starting to fade from her memory. In fact, she had almost convinced herself that they had been some sort of reaction to the arrival of that poison pen letter. Everyone knew that delayed shock could affect people in a dozen different ways. Well, she had reacted by becoming emotionally unstable for a while. She was all right now, though. She was over it, and gradually getting back to her old self.

To her relief, Julius stayed away from her. She ate her meals alone, and only caught a fleeting glimpse of him all day as he disappeared through a far doorway.

When Jessamy finally went up to bed that night, she was tired, but pleased with the way that the day had gone. She thought she might even be able to get a good night's sleep for the first time since she had arrived at the house.

A long shower relaxed her still further. She pulled

on a short silk nightdress—a rather extravagant Christmas present from one of her sisters—brushed her hair until the long dark strands gleamed, then walked slowly over to the window.

It was a clear night, with a full moon shining brightly out of the velvet sky. She was finally beginning to get used to the silence, although she still missed the noise and buzz of the city. She didn't think she was ever going to be completely converted to a country girl.

She yawned, and decided it was time to go to bed. She was just about to turn away from the window when she thought she saw something suddenly move in the far corner of the walled garden.

She peered out into the darkness, but it was difficult to see anything very clearly. Even after she had switched off the small lamp beside the bed, so that the room was completely dark, it was hard to be sure if she was really seeing something, or if her eyes were just playing tricks.

'It's probably only one of the local kids sneaking in for a look around,' Jessamy tried to reassure herself. But on the other hand, it could be someone planning to break in. Burglaries didn't only happen in London.

What should she do? she wondered uneasily. Call the local police? But she would look rather a fool if it did turn out to be only one of the children from the village. What was the alternative, though? Creep down, armed with a poker, and confront the intruder?

Jessamy gave a small grimace. She didn't think she was the stuff that heroines were made of! On the other hand, she supposed she couldn't just ignore it.

She stared out of the window again, but this time couldn't see any movement at all.

'Perhaps you were mistaken,' she told herself hopefully. 'Why not go to bed and forget about it?'

Then she gave a small sigh. She knew she couldn't do that. She would just lie awake half the night with her conscience pricking guiltily, and that would be a nuisance, because she really needed some sleep.

She finally decided that she would go down to the garden and take a closer look. If there wasn't any sign of anyone, then she could go back to bed and sleep peacefully. And if there *was* someone there, then she definitely didn't intend to do anything brave. She would run, or yell very loudly—or perhaps both!

She pulled on her towelling bathrobe and slid her feet into a pair of sandals. Then she opened the bedroom door and crept down through the dark, silent house.

As she let herself out into the garden through the kitchen door, she gave a small shiver that had absolutely nothing to do with the autumnal chill in the air. Her soft-soled sandals didn't make a sound as she crossed the terrace, then she began to make her way through the walled garden, towards the corner where she thought she had seen something—or someone— move.

Now that she was actually out here in the dark, on her own, it occurred to her that this really wasn't a good idea at all. In fact, it was downright foolish. What if someone jumped out at her? Attacked her? Coshed her? As all the alarming possibilities ran through her head, she gave a loud gulp and came to an abrupt halt. She nervously decided that she didn't want to go any further. If someone was lurking in the garden, then they could stay there. She wasn't going to disturb them!

She turned round, ready to scuttle back to the house,

and immediately cannoned into a hard, warm body.
She yelled out loud, then shouted again as strong
fingers closed round her arms.

'It's a good thing we don't have any close neigh-
bours,' remarked Julius's voice. 'If we did, they'd all
have been awake by now!'

Jessamy hurriedly wriggled free of her husband's
grip. 'What are *you* doing here?' she demanded.

'I was about to ask you the same question.'

'I thought I saw something moving about in the
garden.'

Julius's eyes immediately darkened. 'You mean an
intruder?'

'I don't really know,' she admitted. 'It could have
been just a bush moving in the breeze. Or an animal.'

'Where did you see it?'

'Over there.' She pointed towards the far corner of
the walled garden.

'Wait here,' he said at once. 'I'll go and check.'

'On your own?'

His dark eyebrows rose gently. 'Are you volunteering to come with me?'

'No,' she said, with a small shiver. 'Sorry, but I'm
definitely a coward when it comes to this sort of thing.'

'Then what are you doing out here in the first place?'

'I don't really know,' she admitted. 'I suppose I came
down on impulse, but as soon as I got here I wished I'd
stayed in the house. This garden is eerie at night!
Things rustle in the dark, and everything's shadowy
and spooky.'

'Then stay right here while I go and take a look.'

He strode off into the darkness, and Jessamy gave a
resigned shake of her head. There were times when
Julius was so very Taurean. Without any hesitation, he

had gone off to confront a possible intruder. And if he found one and the situation turned ugly, Jessamy knew who she would put her money on!

It seemed like ages before he came back again, and when he did, she pounced on him.

'What did you find?' she demanded.

'Nothing,' he told her. 'It was probably a fox moving around in the bushes, or perhaps even a badger. When you yelled so loudly, they almost certainly bolted.'

'Well, you shouldn't have grabbed me like that,' she said crossly. 'Anyway, how did you know I was out here?'

'I heard the kitchen door open and close. When I looked out of the window and saw you creeping through the garden, I thought I'd better come down and find out what you were up to.'

'What did you think I was doing?' she said a little irritably. 'A moonlight flit? Getting away from you while you were safely tucked up in bed?'

'No, I didn't think that,' he said equably. 'Not many people run away wearing just a bathrobe.' Then his voice changed and this time held a warning note. 'Anyway, I think you understand very well that leaving here wouldn't be a wise thing to do. Not wise at all.'

'Oh, yes, I understand that!' she retorted with a sudden rush of fresh bitterness. 'If I do try and run away, then you're going to make sure I'm hounded by the press.'

'Precisely,' Julius agreed.

'I ought to call your bluff,' she muttered. 'I don't believe anyone—not even you—would carry out a threat like that.'

'Believe it,' he advised softly.

Her blue eyes glowed with a rebellious light.

'Why should I?'

'Because I'd do anything to keep you here, Jessamy.'

And once Julius had made his mind up about something, Jessamy knew only too well that he never changed it. But *why* did he want to keep her here? Especially since she had made it very clear that she didn't want to stay.

Without any warning, she found herself remembering how Julius's body had felt when she had cannoned into it, just minutes ago. Hard, warm and, most frightening of all, so *familiar*. It was the first physical contact between them for four years, but for just an instant it had seemed as if it had only been yesterday when she had last touched him.

Jessamy discovered that she had begun to tremble. Instinctively, she pulled the bathrobe around her more tightly, and took a step backwards.

'You're always retreating from me,' murmured Julius.

'Of course I am,' she said in a voice that was sharp with nerves. 'It's because I don't want you anywhere near me!'

She expected an angry response, and it rather unnerved her when it didn't come.

'You never used to feel like that,' he said instead. 'Do you remember how it used to be between us, Jessamy?' he went on in that same low and almost hypnotic voice.

'I've spent the last four years learning how to forget it,' she retorted edgily. 'And I've succeeded. I *don't* remember how it used to be between us, Julius.'

This time she did get a response. And it was so swift that there was absolutely nothing she could do to avoid it.

'Then let me remind you,' Julius said in a very different tone of voice. And almost before he had finished speaking, his mouth forced itself over hers in a kiss that was clearly designed to punish her for that last remark.

Jessamy fought it silently and grimly. It was impossible to get away from him, though, so in desperation she resorted to other tactics. She froze him out; went limp in his arms and let her lips go slack under his. She wanted him to feel as if he were kissing a lifeless rag doll.

'Don't do that to me!' he muttered angrily. He kissed her again and, as her flesh remained slack and dead, his voice changed and suddenly sounded a little desperate. 'Jessamy—please—don't do it.'

The ragged plea hit a nerve that seemed connected to her soul. Her mouth slowly stirred under his and Jessamy knew she was making a big, big mistake, but it seemed impossible to stop.

Her memory stirred along with her body, and everything came tumbling back into her mind with an overwhelming rush. She had never really forgotten any of it, of course, how could she forget something that had consumed her so completely, even if it had lasted such a short time? Instead, she had pushed the memories into a dark cupboard in the very farthest corner of her mind, and she had thought they were safely locked away, only now Julius had found the key and he was *opening* the cupboard.

Memories tumbled out, dancing past her closed eyes in a vivid string of pictures. Julius kissing her, Julius licking and nibbling at her skin, Julius's fingers moving over her in a series of inquisitive caresses that were so pleasurable they almost hurt. He had introduced her to physical passion, and at the same time ignited a fire in his own sensual, earthy Taurean nature that had proved impossible to quench.

Her heart thumped painfully as she remembered him making love to her for the first time, the hard, forceful thrust of his body coming much quicker than she had expected, an abrupt shock after all the gentleness that had gone before. But, even with all his experience, he hadn't been able to wait, and it hadn't mattered, nothing had been important then except being together.

Now his kiss threatened to start it all over again. Except it was different this time, Jessamy reminded herself as she pulled herself slowly and painfully back to reality. Everything was behind them and the future didn't exist. And this kiss was meaningless, because there was nothing behind it; it was only the last flickering spark of something they had destroyed a long time ago.

Julius slowly lifted his head. 'Do you hate me?' he said thickly.

'For a long time I hated you very much,' she said slowly. 'Now I simply don't think of you at all.' She didn't tell him that was the only way she had been able to cope with his absence, by blocking him out completely and refusing even to acknowledge his existence.

He drew in a long, shuddering breath. 'You make me feel as if I'd died.'

She wasn't cruel enough to tell him that there had been times when she had almost wished he had. In an odd way, that might have been easier to bear.

He moved away from her. 'Do you expect me to apologise for all this?' he asked in a rough voice.

Suddenly very tired, she shook her head. 'Let's just try and forget it.'

'Forget it!' Julius repeated with abrupt vehemence. 'That's your solution to everything, isn't it? Forget it, wipe it out, pretend it never happened. But what if you *can't* forget? What's your solution then, Jessamy?'

'I don't know,' she muttered. 'I don't think I have one.'

'And nor do I.' He moved restlessly. 'Go on back to the house,' he said, in a voice that suddenly sounded as weary as hers.

'Will you be all right?' She had no idea what had made her blurt that out.

Julius's mouth twisted in a strained, totally humour-less smile. 'No, I won't be all right. But that isn't your problem, is it? Go away, Jessamy,' he ordered.

And since there didn't seem anything she could do, and there wasn't anything else she dared to say, she turned round and slowly trudged back to the house. She had forgotten why she had come down to the garden in the first place. Forgotten that she had thought she had seen someone moving around in the darkness.

But she hadn't forgotten the kiss that Julius had given her. He was right, some things could never be wiped from the memory.

Jessamy felt the touch of his lips again and shivered deeply, as if someone had just walked over her grave.

CHAPTER FIVE

THAT nerve-racking encounter with Julius had dashed any hopes Jessamy had ever had of being able to get a good night's sleep.

When she got back to her room, she bolted the door with fumbling fingers, then paced round and round. She was too restless to stay still for even a moment, but too tired to be able to think straight.

At one point she roamed over to the window and gazed out. The first thing she saw, though, was Julius walking slowly back to the house. For a few seconds, she just stared at him. She couldn't seem to drag her eyes away from his familiar figure.

As if he could suddenly feel her looking at him, he glanced directly up at her window. Jessamy jumped back as quickly as if she had been shot. She didn't want him to know that she had been looking at him. In fact, there were so many things she didn't want him to know that a list of them would have stretched on and on.

After a while she forced herself to stop wandering around the room and instead got into bed. She had to get some rest or she was going to fall apart. Or perhaps she was falling apart already, she thought a little wildly, and she just hadn't realised it.

She spent the next couple of hours staring into the darkness. She couldn't even bring herself to close her eyes. Then a sudden wave of exhaustion swept over her, and she slid into a light doze. Soon, though, she began to dream—confused, disturbing dreams, and all of them about Julius. The past and present were muddled together, he was kissing her and then shouting at her, kissing her again and then coldly ignoring her. Then more sensual images slid through her unconscious mind, and she felt Julius's hands against her skin, the heat and hardness of his body as he slid closer——

Jessamy woke up with a sudden start. She ached inside, a sensation that had once been very familiar, but which she had deliberately suppressed over the last four years until she had almost forgotten what it had felt like. She remembered it now, though! With a low groan, she thumped the pillow with a mixture of anger and frustration. Before she had come here, she had had her life sorted out and everything had been running smoothly. All right, so it wasn't perfect, but nothing ever was. She had been getting though the days—and nights—without too many problems, and there had been times when she had almost felt happy.

But now things had begun to go badly wrong. It had started with the arrival of that poison pen letter, and ended with that kiss. Only she had the awful feeling that wasn't the end of it at all, and that was the *really* scary part of all this.

She curled up into a small ball, too tired to stay awake, but too scared to go to sleep in case she started to dream again. In the end, she catnapped, shaking herself awake every time she felt herself drifting towards a deeper sleep.

By the time morning finally came she felt like a total wreck. She crawled out of bed, peered into the mirror, and gave a small groan. She also *looked* like a total wreck!

A long shower only improved things fractionally. Make-up might have helped, but she hadn't bothered to bring any with her. Her skin was still lightly tanned from the summer, her thick dark eyelashes didn't need mascara to give them extra body, and the blue of her eyes and the dusky pink of her lips usually gave her face enough colour.

This morning, though, she looked completely washed out. Even the dark fall of her hair seemed to have lost its gloss.

'It's probably a good thing,' she muttered to herself. 'Julius will take one look at you and wonder why he ever bothered to kiss you last night.'

As soon as she said Julius's name out loud, she shivered. Oh, this was ridiculous! she told herself in a deeply shaken voice. A kiss wasn't important. It was just something that sometimes happened. There was nothing deeply significant about it. She certainly didn't need to get wound up about it, especially as it was fairly certain it wouldn't happen again. In fact, she would make very sure it didn't.

Even after she was fully dressed, she lingered in the bedroom for another hour. Then she suddenly got very annoyed with herself. She was twenty-four, she was an adult, and she had become very competent at coping with life. She didn't need to hide away in her room like a schoolgirl who was frightened of facing the world.

She opened the door and marched downstairs with new determination. As she went through the hall, though, she glanced out of the front windows, and gave a loud groan as she saw Eleanor's car parked on the drive outside.

'Oh, great!' she muttered. 'That's all I need!'

She decided to head straight for the drawing-room at the back of the house, where she worked. That way, she should be able to avoid both Eleanor and Julius.

As she hurried towards the door at the far end of the hall, though, it opened and Eleanor walked in.

Julius's secretary stopped dead when she saw Jessamy.

'I see you're still here,' she said, in a very cool voice.

'It certainly looks like it,' agreed Jessamy. 'What are *you* doing here this morning? More urgent papers for Julius?'

'There were a couple of things I thought needed to be dealt with straight away.'

'So you brought them in person.' Jessamy's blue eyes glittered briefly. 'What a very conscientious secretary you are!'

'I try to be as efficient as possible.'

'Yes, I know. But that's where you've made your big mistake, Eleanor.' Jessamy allowed her voice to become deliberately sympathetic as she looked at the older woman. 'You see, Julius doesn't like efficiency in his private life. I know that's hard to believe, because you'd think he'd choose a wife who's always well-dressed, competent at absolutely everything, and totally reliable. Those are only the qualities he looks for in the people who work for him, though. At home, he simply wants to feel relaxed and comfortable. He isn't particularly interested in an active social life, and he certainly doesn't believe in mixing business and pleasure. In fact, he likes a very casual lifestyle—and I'm afraid you're not a very casual person, Eleanor,' she finished.

'And, of course, you are,' Eleanor said icily.

Jessamy glanced down at her paint-stained jeans. 'I certainly dress casually,' she agreed wryly.

But Eleanor hadn't finished yet. 'If you think you know Julius so well, and you're sure *you're* the kind of person he wants, then tell me something,' she said with soft malice. 'Why weren't you able to keep him for more than a few months?'

Eleanor's perfectly shaped mouth registered a small smile of triumph as the colour slowly filtered from Jessamy's face.

That was definitely a blow below the belt! Jessamy decided rather shakily. Perhaps it wasn't a good idea to launch into open warfare against someone like Eleanor. It was just that the woman *irritated* her so much. Chasing after Julius in that oh, so subtle and ladylike way, looking down that elegant nose of hers at Jessamy because she didn't wear designer clothes or lead a sophisticated social life, silently sneering at her because she had lost Julius just as she, Eleanor, had always predicted she would.

'You look a total mess this morning,' Eleanor went on coolly, obviously feeling that all the advantages were piling up on her side. 'Don't you have any decent clothes? Or ever visit a hairdresser? And you're obviously not sleeping well. You look quite haggard.' Jessamy was about to fling an equally rude reply straight back at her, but Eleanor's gaze suddenly moved past Jessamy and her face changed completely. 'Good morning, Julius,' she said, in a very different tone of voice.

Jessamy hadn't heard her husband walk into the hall. She turned round slowly, not at all sure she was ready to face him.

She found that his dark brown gaze was already fixed on her, and she swallowed very hard. Julius stared at her for what seemed like an extraordinarily long time. Then his eyes finally flicked back to his secretary.

'What are you doing here, Eleanor?' he said, very curtly.

'There were some papers I thought you ought to see. They relate to the takeover of Matthews Construction.'

Julius took them from her, rifled through them, then gave a hard frown. 'These aren't particularly urgent. They could easily have waited for a few days.'

'I'm sorry,' Eleanor said smoothly. 'I thought you wanted to see all papers relating to that takeover straight away. Now that I'm here, though, do you want me to stay and get on with some work?'

Nice try, Eleanor, thought Jessamy almost admiringly. You had to give the woman full marks for persistence. She never lost an opportunity to push herself right under Julius's nose. What a pity he never even seemed to notice she was there!

'I don't have any urgent work outstanding,' Julius said dismissively. 'You can go straight back to the office. You'll be far more use to me there.'

His gaze had already returned to Jessamy, and she suddenly realised she didn't want to be left alone with Julius.

'It's a tiring drive back to London,' she said quickly. 'Perhaps Eleanor would like a cup of coffee before she leaves?'

Eleanor immediately looked surprised. She obviously hadn't expected Jessamy to provide her with an excuse for staying longer at the house.

Julius growled something under his breath. Obviously, being even marginally civil was an effort this morning. 'I suppose Eleanor can stay for coffee,' he muttered at last.

'Are you going to join us?' invited Eleanor, with a

smile that would have charmed most men right into the palm of her hand.

Julius didn't even seem to notice it. 'I've other things to do.' He began to stride off, but stopped when he drew level with Jessamy.

'You look good this morning,' he said in a low voice. 'I'd almost forgotten how good you look in the mornings.' Then he quickly left the hall before she had the chance to reply.

Jessamy hoped Eleanor hadn't heard those last remarks. Unfortunately, there was absolutely nothing wrong with the older woman's hearing.

Eleanor's cold green gaze locked on to Jessamy's face. 'He's absolutely blind where you're concerned, isn't he?' she said with a disbelieving shake of her head. 'You're his one weakness. He'd be much more a man if he'd never met you.'

'Perhaps everyone should have a weakness,' Jessamy said slowly. 'It makes us more human—more likeable.'

'You've done nothing for him except wreck his life. If Julius needed a weakness, then it certainly wasn't you.'

But Jessamy had suddenly had quite enough of the older woman's interference. Blue eyes glowing, she rounded on her.

'Whatever I've done or haven't done to Julius, it's really none of your business, is it? You're just his secretary, and that's all you're ever going to be. Either you've got to decide to settle for that, or you should clear out of his life altogether.'

Jessamy knew her words were cruel, but she felt as if she had been pushed very near to her limit. Even in the early days of her marriage to Julius, Eleanor had always seemed to be there in the background. She would ring Julius at home, with messages that were only just important enough for her to justify ringing his private number. And when Jessamy had tried to speak to Julius at his office, Eleanor had always been on the other end of the phone, trotting out some barely plausible excuse why Julius couldn't talk to her. She had been like a barrier between Jessamy and her husband, not particularly important but always *there*, irritating and chafing, like a stone in the shoe.

'He won't take you back,' Eleanor said now, with absolute certainty. 'He might find it hard to look at you objectively, but he isn't stupid. He isn't going to put himself through all that again.'

'I don't want him back!' Jessamy retorted. 'Anyway, do you think the break-up was easy for me?'

Eleanor shrugged. 'You seem to have dealt with it without too many problems. You've got a career, a home, and you've probably had plenty of men in your life.'

'And of course Julius has lived like an absolute monk for the last four years,' Jessamy threw back at her angrily. 'The gossip columnists simply invented all those stories about the women he's been seen with!'

She was immediately angry with herself for admitting to Eleanor that she had read those newspaper items, and that they had got to her. In fact, this entire conversation was getting out of hand. She fervently wished she had never started it.

'Why don't you just get out of here?' she muttered. 'Go back to London.'

'Don't worry, I'm going,' Eleanor said calmly. 'I only came back because I wanted to take another look at you, to see if you'd really changed. And you haven't, Jessamy. Five years ago when you married Julius, you were the wrong person for him, and you're still the wrong person. I don't need to worry about you. You're never going to be a permanent part of Julius's life.'

'I don't even want to be,' Jessamy threw back at her, just a little too fiercely. 'And I'm beginning to realise that you're a rather sick person, Eleanor. All these years you've spent chasing after something you know you can't have. Only a real masochist would spend their life doing something like that. I mean, what do you get out of it? You know you're never going to be anything more than Julius's secretary.'

'Perhaps that's enough for me,' said Eleanor, her voice still unruffled.

'It can't be!'

'Why not? At least I get to spend almost every day with him. Even when you were first married to Julius, I saw more of your husband than you ever did. And during the last four years you haven't seen him at all, while I've spent nine or ten hours a day with him, sometimes even more if we're particularly busy. I travel abroad with him, I help him to organise his business life, and I'm always there if he needs me. So tell me, Jessamy, who do you think is closer to Julius? You or me?'

Eleanor's words absolutely stunned her. She supposed she had never before realised just how much time Eleanor and Julius spent together, or how close their work brought them. Jessamy was horrified to find that a wave of pure jealousy was beginning to sweep through her. Terrified that it might show on her face, she quickly turned away.

'I've got work to do,' she said in a voice so brittle that it threatened to crack completely. 'If you want some coffee before you leave, go to the kitchen and make it yourself. Otherwise, just get out of here. I think you've outstayed your welcome, Eleanor.'

She hurried out of the hall as soon as she had finished speaking, not even particularly caring if it looked as if she were running away. Instinctively, she headed for the door that led out into the garden. This house suddenly felt as if it were suffocating her. She had to get out into the fresh air.

She hurried through the door, then dragged in several lungfuls of the clean, sweet air. The wall of the house was behind her and she leant back against the warm brickwork and closed her eyes. That wave of jealousy had really scared her half to death. Any kind of emotional response connected to Julius frightened her senseless. To stay completely safe, she had to feel absolutely nothing about him at all.

'Has Eleanor gone?' asked Julius's voice a little roughly, from only a few feet way.

Jessamy opened her eyes, then swiftly closed them again as she saw his tall figure standing there. Oh no! she thought miserably. She didn't want to see him right now. In fact, this was a totally disastrous time for her to come face to face with him.

'What's the matter?' Julius went on more sharply. 'Aren't you feeling well?'

She managed to force her eyes open again. 'I'm feeling fine,' she said in a cracked voice.

'You don't look it. And you don't sound it.' His dark eyes narrowed. 'Did Eleanor say something to upset you?'

'No—yes—it isn't important,' she muttered, wishing he would just *go away*.

'I didn't ask her to come here this morning.'

'I know that.'

'But I did deliberately bring her here yesterday,' Julius went on.

Her eyes began to focus on him more attentively. 'Of course you brought her here,' she said a little warily. 'You had work to do, and there were important files and papers that you needed.'

'She didn't bring me anything of outstanding urgency,' he said. 'I could have left those papers for another three or four days before dealing with them.'

Jessamy became very still. 'Then why did you ask her to come to the house?'

He was looking at her very intently now. She didn't like it, but she couldn't back away without making it very obvious that her nerve-ends were definitely reacting to his closeness.

'I remembered that you never liked Eleanor,' Julius said in a soft voice. 'Just mentioning her name was always enough to make you bristle. I began to wonder if she'd still have the same effect on you.'

She stared at him in growing disbelief. 'You brought her here just to find out if I still disliked her? What on earth did you do that for?'

A shadow of a smile touched the corners of his mouth, giving it an unexpectedly sensual line. Jessamy swallowed hard and silently ordered herself to ignore his mouth completely, no matter what line or mood it moulded itself into.

Julius seemed to be relaxing a little now. 'You really don't know? You haven't figured it out yet? You always used to be a lot quicker than this, Jessamy.'

'Well, I've changed a lot over the past four years,' she retorted. 'In fact, I've changed completely.'

'I'm beginning to think you haven't changed at all.'

That last dangerous statement seemed to hang in the sunlit air between them for a very long time.

Jessamy could feel her throat going dry, and forced herself to swallow. She didn't want her voice to come out in a dry croak.

'I'm not the same person at all,' she insisted, and was very relieved to find that her voice sounded quite convincing.

'But that's the whole point,' Julius pointed out smoothly. 'If you've changed so much, then you shouldn't care in the least whether Eleanor's here or not. She shouldn't mean anything to you at all.'

Jessamy began to realise what he was getting at. She also began to realise that she might have made a very big mistake.

'Do you know why you disliked Eleanor so much five years ago, when we were first married?' Julius went on. 'It was because you instinctively recognised her as a rival. Not a serious rival, of course, but you knew she spent a lot of time with me, and part of you resented that. And she'd already been with me for several years before we met, so you felt that perhaps she knew me better than you did, and you hated that.'

'Rubbish,' muttered Jessamy. 'I just didn't like her, that was all. Feelings like that are instinctive. And they don't just fade away, they stay with you. That's why I *still* don't like her.'

'And jealousy has absolutely nothing to do with it?'

'*Jealousy*?' she repeated, putting as much incredulity into her voice as she could manage. 'Do you think I'm jealous of Eleanor because she's spent the last four years with you, and I haven't?'

Again she knew at once that she had said the wrong

thing. If she had really been as indifferent as she had pretended to be, then she wouldn't have reacted at all.

Julius's dark brown eyes held an odd gleam of triumph, as if he had realised exactly the same thing.

'Bringing Eleanor here was a good idea,' he murmured. 'It's told me things that you'd never have admitted in a hundred years.'

'What do you mean?' Jessamy said edgily.

He came a step nearer. 'Almost as soon as you saw her, you began to argue with her. She still gets to you, doesn't she, Jessamy? And that's because *I* still get to you.'

'No!' she shot back at once.

He ignored her denial. 'Just as that kiss last night got to you,' he went on relentlessly.

'That kiss meant nothing,' Jessamy lied furiously.

His mouth curled into a dark smile. 'I don't believe you. But you can try and convince me, if you like.'

'I don't have to convince you of anything!'

'I think you do.' His eyes were changing colour, from rich brown to almost black.

'All right, how do I convince you?' she challenged him rashly.

'That's easy.' The dark smile became more pronounced. 'We'll try that kiss all over again, and you can show me just how indifferent you are.'

But Jessamy wasn't about to go along with that. Quite apart from anything else, she had serious doubts about how indifferent she could remain if Julius came any closer.

'Oh, no,' she said at once. 'I told you, I'm not playing games with you. And particularly not this kind of game.'

'Why not? Scared?' he taunted gently.

Jessamy decided she had had more than enough of this. 'Leave me alone, Julius!' she said tautly.

'I wish I could.'

Something in his tone of voice made her look at him with new wariness.

'What do you mean by that?'

His eyes were glowing intently now. 'I wish I could forget you. Wish I were indifferent to you. Wish I were all the things that you're pretending to be.'

'I'm *not* pretending,' she said fiercely.

'You can easily prove it.' His dark gaze fixed on her challengingly. 'Just one kiss, Jessamy, that's all it'll take.'

But she didn't dare let him any closer. 'Why are you doing this?' she said in a low voice.

'Haven't you figured it out yet?'

She shook her head slowly. 'I don't understand *any* of this.'

'It's very easy,' Julius said evenly. 'It's taken me four years to get to the point where I can admit this, but I still want you, Jessamy. And you know I never give up on something I want.'

Her eyes flew wide open, then her face became white with anger. 'You can't have me! I'm not something you can pick up and put down whenever you feel like it.' Her blue eyes flared fiercely. 'I've learnt a lot during the time we've been apart, Julius. I know now that you're very good at making love, but no good at being *in* love. You keep all your feelings buried too deeply, you can't—or won't—show them. You hate to give up on anything, though, so even now you won't *admit* that our marriage was a failure. It was, though, and you're going to have to learn to live with that fact, because you're certainly not going to get a chance to put it right!'

With that, she turned round and ran back into the house. Without really thinking where she was going, she headed blindly towards her room. Once inside, she slammed the door in a sudden fit of pure anger.

How dared he do this to her? Try and resurrect something that was well and truly dead! And she was equally furious with herself for letting things get so out of hand. She should have turned and walked away as soon as the conversation began to get so very personal.

While she was muttering to herself, she was emptying drawers and cupboards, and throwing her things into her suitcase. She must have been mad to let him bring her here, even madder to have stayed. He wouldn't have carried out those threats to set the press on her. Julius was too civilised.

Then Jessamy gave a sudden shiver. While they had been talking, there had been a couple of moments when he hadn't looked in the least civilised!

That didn't stop her chucking the last of her things into the case, though. She was just pushing down the lid and trying to close the catches with fumbling fingers when the door swung open.

Julius stood in the doorway, and there was a bright light in his eyes that made her feel very alarmed.

'What are you doing?' he said in a voice that sounded unnaturally calm.

'I'd have thought that was fairly obvious,' Jessamy retorted.

'You're packing,' he stated flatly.

'I'm not just packing. I'm leaving!'

'No, you're not.'

She whirled round to face him. 'Going to threaten

me again?' she enquired sarcastically. 'Well, it won't work, Julius. I know you. You won't set the press on me. You'd never actually do anything like that.'

He came further into the room. 'If you believe that, why did you stay here in the first place?'

'Because I thought you might have changed. I thought you might have become the sort of man who *would* do something like that.'

He looked at her very steadily. 'I have changed. And believe me when I tell you that I'll do whatever I have to do to make you stay here.'

'Why is it so important that I stay?' she demanded. 'That's what I don't understand!'

'Yes, you do,' he replied, his gaze never leaving her face. 'You're beginning to understand it very well.'

Jessamy gave an involuntary shiver because she was afraid he was right. At long last, she was beginning to realise why she was here.

'It won't do you any good to keep me here,' she said at last, in a dull voice. 'You can't have me, Julius. It won't ever be the same as it was.'

'I know that. And I don't want it to be the same.'

'Then what do you want?' she burst out in a sudden rush of frustration. 'What is this all about?'

Julius seemed very much in control of himself again now. The bright light had left his eyes and his face was set into determined lines.

'It's about getting a little of my sanity back again.'

'You don't need me to do that!'

'Oh, but I do,' he said in a soft voice. 'That's why I intend to keep you here.'

Jessamy stared at him defiantly. 'And what if I simply walk out, and to hell with the consequences?'

He looked back at her levelly. 'You won't do that.

For one thing, you're not the only one who'll be affected if I give that story about the poison pen letter to the press. What about your family, Jessamy? You've always been very close to them—in fact, it's one of the things I envied about you. How do you think *they'd* feel if they saw details of your private life splashed all over the tabloids?'

She had to fight back tears of frustration because, of course, he was right. She would absolutely hate it if she had to submit her family to that sort of ordeal. And she kept trying to convince herself that Julius would never carry out his threat, but it had been four very long years that they had been apart. What if he had become much more ruthless in that time? She already knew how very bull-headed he could be when he was going after something he wanted.

'Are you sure you didn't send that poison pen letter yourself?' she muttered, her blue eyes flashing. 'Just so that you'd have a good excuse for keeping me a prisoner here?'

Julius looked directly at his wife. 'No, I didn't send you that letter,' he told her, quite truthfully. 'If you remember, I tried to stop you even seeing it. I didn't want you to be hurt.'

Jessamy's blue eyes suddenly blazed. 'You didn't want me to be hurt? Four years ago you walked out on me!' she yelled at him angrily. 'Do you think *that* didn't hurt me?'

'You made it impossible for me to stay,' he said rather tightly.

'*I* made it impossible?' she echoed incredulously.

He made an effort to hold on to his temper. 'Jessamy, I don't want to fight with you. Perhaps we should try showing a little tolerance towards each other. That way, we might be able to achieve something over the next couple of days.'

But Jessamy wasn't in the mood to be placated. 'I don't want to achieve anything,' she hissed at him. 'And I certainly don't feel tolerant!'

He still managed to keep his temper in check.

'Then it would obviously be best if I leave you on your own until you're in a more reasonable mood,' he said, walking towards the door.

'I'm not going to feel in the least reasonable while you're forcing me to stay in this house,' she warned fiercely.

He reached the doorway, turned, and gave a grim smile. 'I don't really care how you feel. The important thing is that you're here—with me.'

He left immediately after that. Jessamy's temper gradually faded away and in its place came a deep feeling of unease.

What had he meant by that last remark? she wondered, her skin prickling with tension. What was Julius up to? What did he want from her?

Whatever it was, he wasn't going to get it! She had survived for four years without him; she didn't need him any more.

Julius was about to learn that his wife had developed a mind and a will of her own. She had fought hard to make a new life for herself—and there was absolutely no room in it for her husband.

CHAPTER SIX

JESSAMY spent the rest of the day deliberately avoiding Julius. It wasn't too difficult. He seemed to have meant it when he had told her he would leave her on her own until she was in a more reasonable frame of mind.

For a while she tried to work, but it was useless. Her drawings were flat and unimaginative. She tore them up and tossed them into the bin.

After an early evening meal, she retreated to her room. Her suitcase was still sitting on the bed, with the few clothes and belongings she had brought with her piled into it. She stared at it for a couple of minutes, then, with a prolonged sigh, began to take them out and put them back into the cupboards and drawers.

Although she hadn't expected to, she actually managed to sleep for a few hours that night. It didn't seem to help in any way, though. She woke up in the morning feeling heavy-eyed and with a dull headache lurking behind her eyes.

She picked unenthusiastically at the breakfast she made for herself, and afterwards wandered out into the garden. Only a slight chill in the air gave any indication that it was autumn, and even that was beginning to fade away as the sun blazed down again out of a clear blue sky. Jessamy shaded her aching eyes from its brightness, and wished it would rain. She wanted the weather to be gloomy and overcast, with lots of black clouds to match her mood.

'Are you in a more friendly mood this morning?' Julius enquired, moving silently up behind her.

Jessamy jumped violently. She hadn't seen or heard him approach.

'I wish you'd leave me alone,' she muttered.

'I wish I could,' he replied softly.

She spun round to face him, her mouth already setting into an angry line. 'Don't start all that again! I'm not in the mood for it.'

Julius studied her face. 'No, you're not, are you?' he said at last. 'What's wrong?'

'Do you really need to ask me that?' she said incredulously. 'I've got a headache, I'm stuck here in this damned house, you keep following me around and annoying me, and on top of that I can't work!'

'Why can't you work?'

'It might have something to do with the fact that there are too many distractions!' she retorted.

Julius looked at her thoughtfully. 'Does that include me?'

She was about to retort that it most certainly did, but then hurriedly stopped herself. If she did that, she would be admitting that he still had the power to affect her, and she wasn't going to do that!

'Certainly not,' she said stiffly.

He didn't actually call her a liar out loud, but it was clear that he didn't believe her. That really annoyed Jessamy. She glared at him, and began to turn away.

'Perhaps you ought to spend a few hours away from the house,' Julius suggested, before she had time to stalk off.

'I thought you wanted to keep me here?' she retorted. 'That I wasn't meant to set foot outside the house and grounds?'

'Don't be ridiculous,' he said calmly. 'You can go out whenever you please—as long as you come back again.' He reached into his pocket and took out some keys. 'Do you want to borrow my car?'

Jessamy gave a dark scowl. 'I still can't drive.'

His eyebrows shot up. 'I thought you would have learnt by now.'

'There never seemed to be any time,' she said defensively.

'How do you get around?'

'There are such things as buses and trains,' she reminded him with a touch of sarcasm. 'And I've got a bicycle.'

'A car would be more practical.'

'And a lot more expensive.'

Julius's eyes narrowed. 'You've got money problems?'

She tried not to think of her overdrawn bank account and the credit cards she mustn't use. 'No more than anyone else living in London. It's an expensive place,' she said rather defiantly.

'What kind of money do you earn from your illustrations?'

'Enough. In fact, I'm doing quite well at the moment.'

'You'd have been able to live very comfortably if you'd taken the money I offered, after we separated,' he pointed out.

'I didn't want to live comfortably,' Jessamy retorted. 'I wanted to live independently!'

'At least no one could ever accuse you of being a fortune-hunter,' he said with a ghost of a smile.

Jessamy didn't smile back at him. She was sure his

parents had thought she was precisely that, when he had first taken her home to meet them.

'I don't care in the least about money,' she said flatly. 'Perhaps that's why I never seem to have any,' she added in a more resigned voice.

'Are you still giving away large chunks of your income to ill-treated animals, orphaned children and projects that are going to save the environment?' asked Julius, in a dry tone.

Jessamy bristled. 'All those things are *important*.'

'Eating and paying the rent is important,' he pointed out.

'I manage to do that as well—most of the time.'

'But not at the moment?'

'It's just a very temporary difficult patch,' she said defiantly.

Julius looked at her. 'Even if you had serious money problems you wouldn't come to me for help, would you?'

'I certainly don't want any of your money,' she insisted. 'But I would like you to tell me *how* I'm meant to get away from this house, if I want to go out. There don't even seem to be any local buses. What on earth do people do around here if they want to go somewhere?'

'If they don't drive, then they ask their husbands to give them a lift. Is there anywhere in particular you want to go?'

'Are there any castles in this area?' she asked.

Julius looked rather surprised. 'Castles?' he repeated.

'My illustrations have got to include a couple of castles,' she explained. 'I keep looking at pictures in books, but none of them seems very inspiring. I need to look at the real thing.'

'There are a couple of castles less than an hour's drive away. Do you want one that's still intact, or a romantic ruin?'

'I'd like to look at both,' Jessamy said. She reconsidered his offer of help and reluctantly decided she might just have to accept it. 'Perhaps you could drop me at the nearest bus stop or railway station,' she added. 'I'll make my own way from there.'

'How will you pay for your ticket?' he enquired gently.

'I'll manage,' she said, with a faint scowl.

'By adding a few more pounds to your overdraft?'

'That's none of your business!' She wished he would stop talking about money—and her temporary lack of it. It made her feel she had been incompetent in handling her affairs, and she didn't like that.

To her relief, Julius dropped the subject. 'Go and get your sketch-pad, pencils and whatever else you need,' he said. 'I'll meet you at the car in five minutes.'

Jessamy was halfway to the drawing-room at the back of the house, where she kept her drawing materials, when she came to a sudden halt. Was this a good idea? she asked herself. Hadn't her plan been to avoid Julius as much as possible while she was here? So what was she doing, accepting a lift in his car?

She was getting out of this house for a while, she told herself with a resigned sigh. Right now, that seemed almost more important than getting away from Julius. Perhaps a few hours away from here would cure the feeling of claustrophobia that was beginning to creep over her. Anyway, Julius seemed in a surprisingly reasonable mood this morning. She felt quite confident of being able to cope with him while he was like this.

When she hurried out to the car, carrying her drawing materials which she had shoved hurriedly into a canvas bag, Julius was already sitting in the driving seat. Jessamy scrambled in beside him, then let out a silent sigh of relief as the car moved swiftly off down the drive, leaving the house behind them.

They drove along the empty country roads, then passed through a couple of small, sleepy villages, the soft golden stone of the houses reflecting the warm sunlight. Then Jessamy let out a sudden squeak.

'Stop!'

Julius brought the car to an abrupt halt, a cloud of dust gently rising up behind them.

'What is it?' he queried with a frown.

'It's a bus stop. You can let me out here.'

Before she could get out of the car, though, he began to drive off again.

'Julius, I want to get the bus,' she said with some annoyance.

'Can you see one?'

'Well—no. But I'm sure one will be along soon.'

'This isn't London,' he reminded her. 'They don't turn up every five minutes. Many of these small villages have only one or two buses a day.'

'Oh,' she said, in a rather subdued voice. Then she looked more determined again. 'You'd better take me to the station, then. I'll catch a train.'

'You *can* catch a train,' he agreed. 'But it won't take you to any of the local castles. The line runs in the wrong direction.'

'Then how am I going to get to these castles?' she asked rather crossly.

'I'm going to take you.'

Jessamy sat in silence for a few seconds while she digested that piece of information. 'All the way there?' she said at last, in a suspicious voice.

'Right to the door,' he agreed. 'Or should I say portcullis?' There was almost a note of amusement in his voice now.

'When we started out, you didn't tell me we'd be going all the way by car,' she said rather accusingly.

'Of course not. If I'd told you that, you wouldn't have come.'

'No, I wouldn't,' she said with some feeling.

Julius glanced at her. 'Is the thought of spending the day with me so bad?'

'I just don't think it's very—wise,' Jessamy said, slightly evasively. 'Not under the cicumstances.'

'And what circumstances are those?' he probed gently.

She shot a black look at him. 'You know very well!'

'Explain them to me, Jessamy.'

But she had no intention of doing any such thing. It would involve talking about things that were far too personal. She might even have to mention the kiss he had given her. No, she decided, it was far safer to stay silent!

Signposts began to appear, telling her they were heading in the direction of Stratford-upon-Avon.

'There aren't any castles in Stratford,' she said suspiciously.

'No, there aren't,' agreed Julius. 'But there are at Warwick and Kenilworth, and we have to go through Stratford to get there.'

A few minutes later they were approaching the outskirts of the town. 'Do you want to visit any of the

usual tourist places?' he asked. 'Shakespeare's birth-
place, Anne Hathaway's cottage, Mary Arden's house?
Or, if you like, we could try and get tickets for a
production of the Royal Shakespeare Company.'

'Do you know which play they're doing?' she asked.

Julius's eyes gleamed briefly. 'I believe it's *Romeo
and Juliet.*'

Jessamy hurriedly shook her head. 'No, thanks,' she
said. She definitely wasn't in the mood for a play about
star-crossed lovers!

Tourists still thronged through Stratford, although
not in such overwhelming numbers as in the spring and
summer. Julius growled under his breath as the traffic
almost ground to a halt.

Jessamy looked happily out of the window, though.
'Cars, people, traffic fumes—lovely,' she said wistfully.
'It's almost like being back in London.'

He looked at her wryly. 'You really are a city girl,
aren't you?'

'I told you I was. Oh, the countryside's very nice,
but I still can't get used to all that peace and quiet. I
want to be able to look out of the window and see
other people. I like joining friends for lunch, and
getting together in the evening for talks and
discussions.'

'You're a very contradictory person,' Julius
commented.

'What do you mean?'

'Anyone looking at you would think you'd be perfectly at home in the country. You dress casually, you
don't care about all the things that make a city tick—
finance, politics, big business—and when you're working, you live in a makebelieve world most of the time.'

Jessamy shrugged. 'Perhaps that's *why* I like living

in the city. Because my work is involved with makebelieve, I want to live somewhere that's lively and very
real. I need the contrast.' She gave a slightly twisted
smile. 'You see, we're complete opposites. You're an
earthy, obstinate Taurus. Country life suits you down
to the ground. I'm a Libran, I like people around me
to talk to and argue with. Our lives just don't fit
together at all.'

Julius looked as if he didn't like the idea of them
being opposites. For the first time since they had left
the house, he seemed rather less relaxed. The traffic
began to move again at that point, though, and to
Jessamy's relief he had to give his attention to the road
ahead.

They left Stratford behind, and headed on towards
Warwick. Jessamy was beginning to find it rather odd
to be having this day out with her husband. To anyone
looking at them, they must seem like a perfectly normal
couple. The situation didn't *feel* in the least normal,
though. Jessamy wished, too late, that she had learned
to drive. Then she would have been free to leave the
house whenever she wanted. She definitely didn't like
the idea of being dependent on Julius to take her
wherever she wanted to go.

As they neared Warwick, Julius followed the signs
that indicated the way to the castle. Soon they were
pulling into the car park. Jessamy heaved her bag of
sketch-pads and pencils off the back seat, then turned
to Julius.

'You can wait here if you like. I probably won't be
too long. I don't want to see inside the castle, I just
want to walk around the outside and sketch anything
that looks interesting.'

'I'll come with you,' Julius said at once.

Jessamy gave a resigned shrug. She hadn't really thought he would agree to stay in the car, but it had been worth a try. She wasn't too worried, though, by the prospect of him being there, right beside her, for the next hour or so. Although not packed with tourists like Stratford, Warwick still attracted its fair share of visitors. There were certainly enough people around to make her feel quite safe.

They walked towards the castle, and Jessamy gazed up at the towers and battlements, and the great walls that loomed above them.

'This really looks like a castle,' she said with some satisfaction. She dug out her sketch-pad. 'I don't like working from pictures in books,' she went on, as her pencil began to skim over the first sheet. 'The illustrations always end up looking flat. I can get a lot more atmosphere if I come to a place like this and actually draw what I see.'

'This castle certainly isn't lacking in atmosphere,' commented Julius. 'The earls of Warwick have been some of the most powerful men in English history. They fought at Agincourt and Crécy, during the Wars of the Roses and the Civil War. They influenced kings, plotted for and against the crown, and sometimes paid for it with their lives.'

Jessamy stopped drawing for a few moments. 'It's funny to sit here in the warm sunshine, and think of all that going on here over the centuries.'

'It certainly makes our own lives seem slightly dull by comparison,' Julius agreed drily.

She lightly raised her eyebrows. 'Your life isn't dull, is it?'

'Not since that poison pen letter arrived,' he said pointedly.

Goosepimples skittered over Jessamy's skin. 'I don't want to talk about that,' she said quickly. 'I can't work if I'm distracted, and the thought of that letter is *very* distracting.'

'And do I distract you as well?' Julius asked softly, his dark eyes suddenly fixing on her.

Jessamy's fingers seemed to become nerveless, and she almost dropped her pencil. 'Of course not,' she said, only not quite quickly enough. She hurriedly got to her feet. 'I've finished sketching this part of the castle,' she muttered. 'Let's move on.'

To her relief, Julius didn't say anything more after that. She spent the next hour wandering round, drawing towers, battlements, gateways, and sections of wall, gradually becoming absorbed again in what she was doing.

The river Avon ran past the foot of the hill on which the castle was situated. Julius strolled over and looked down at the quietly flowing water.

'If we cross to the far side of the river, you'll get a good overall view of the castle,' he pointed out to Jessamy.

She shook her head, though. 'I don't want an overall view. I just want to sketch small sections of it. Then, when I come to do my illustrations, I can put the sections together in whatever combination I like, and come up with a castle of my own.'

'How much longer are you going to be?' Julius glanced at his watch. 'I'm getting hungry.'

'I just want to finish this tower, and that'll be it.'

Jessamy quickly drew in the details, her hand moving with sure confidence over the sheet of paper. Then she shoved the sketch pad back into the bag. 'OK, I'm finished now.'

They walked down towards the town, and Julius finally stopped outside a small restaurant.

'This looks suitable,' he said, and turned towards the entrance.

Jessamy hung back, though. 'Can't we go somewhere a little less—well, expensive?'

'Why?' he asked in surprise.

She glanced down at herself ruefully. 'I'm not exactly dressed for a place like this!'

'Aren't you?' Julius looked at her jeans and T-shirt, as if seeing them for the first time. 'No, I suppose not. As far as I'm concerned, though, clothes aren't important.'

Jessamy pulled a face. 'The owner of the restaurant might have a rather different point of view.' Then she looked at him curiously. 'Would you rather I dressed differently? Wore something smart, with an expensive label?'

He shrugged. 'I really don't think it's important. When I look at you, I see your face, your hair, your skin—just you. Not your clothes.'

She felt her pulses begin to beat in a different rhythm. To disguise her sudden confusion, she said more sharply than she had intended, 'I wish you wouldn't say things like that.'

'I'll say whatever I damned well like.' His own tone had an edge to it now. 'Why shouldn't I, when for the past four years I've been allowed to say nothing at all?'

'Julius, don't!' she said rather angrily. 'Today's been going really well. Don't spoil it.'

His dark eyes began to glow. 'Do you really believe today's been going well? Then you're even more blind than I thought!'

He swung away from her and began to stride off.

Jessamy stood there for a few moments, staring at his retreating back. Then she hurried after him.

'Aren't we going to have something to eat?' she asked as she caught up with him, trying to steer the conversation back on to a safe subject.

'I've lost my appetite,' Julius replied tautly.

'Well, I haven't!'

He dug a couple of notes out of his pocket and thrust them at her.

'Then take this, and go and get yourself some lunch.'

'I'm not going to touch your money,' she said fiercely. 'I've already told you that.'

Julius swung round to face her. 'You won't touch my money—and you won't touch me. Do you know what that makes me feel like? *Do* you?' he repeated harshly.

Jessamy stared at him. 'I don't understand what's going on here,' she said at last. 'One moment everything was fine, and the next it all fell apart. Why, Julius? What's this all about?'

He took a couple of very deep breaths, and the fierce glow gradually faded from his eyes. 'All that happened is that I over-reacted,' he said at last, after a very long pause. His voice sounded more normal now, more controlled. 'I apologise. Do you still want lunch?'

'No,' she said, still staring at him. Food was the very last thing on her mind right now.

'Then let's move on.'

'Move on?' she repeated. 'Where are we going?'

'To Kenilworth. You wanted to see a ruined castle, didn't you?'

'I think I'd sooner go back to the house.'

'We're going to Kenilworth,' Julius repeated, with absolute finality. And Jessamy knew better than to argue with him when he used that particular tone of voice.

They walked back to the car in silence. Julius drove out of Warwick at a speed that was highly illegal, and Jessamy sat tensely beside him, still not understanding why the day had suddenly gone so dangerously wrong.

As if to match the tense atmosphere inside the car, the sun had disappeared behind some ominously black clouds that had crept over the horizon. The air felt storm-charged and Jessamy's nerve-ends responded with a prickling that seemed to warn of danger ahead.

It didn't take them long to reach Kenilworth. The heavy clouds were edging nearer, and Jessamy glanced up uneasily as they got out of the car.

'It looks as if it's going to rain. I don't think it's a good idea to stay here.'

'It isn't going to rain,' Julius said. 'Go ahead and get your sketches done.'

Kenilworth was very different from Warwick; a great red sandstone ruin that almost seemed to glow in the curious half-light as the storm clouds rolled nearer. The great walls, the open windows with their ruined tracery and the crumbling battlements were etched starkly against the darkening sky, and Jessamy had to admit that, seen like this, the castle had a great atmosphere.

She quickly began to sketch, and at the same time tried to imprint on her mind the combination of colours that made the whole scene so eerily effective.

They were the only people still walking around the ruins. The few other tourists who had been here had hurried for cover when they had seen the black sky approaching.

A shaft of lightning suddenly illuminated the scene,

making Jessamy jump. She sketched even faster, wanting to get everything down before it began to pour with rain. A low rumble of thunder made her skin break out in a fine rash of goosepimples, and Julius glanced at her sharply as he noticed them.

'Are you cold?' he asked.

She shook her head. 'No, there's just something about this place that's making my hairs stand on end. Or perhaps it's the storm that's doing it. The castle probably looks quite different in the sunlight.'

'Do you want to come back another day, when the light's better?'

'No,' she said at once. 'This is *exactly* what I need for my illustrations. If I can get just a fraction of this spooky atmosphere into my drawings, then they'll be perfect.'

She wandered on, sketching details of ruined windows, shadowed walls, and towers that had a dark, threatening quality as they were silhouetted against the storm-swollen clouds.

Julius followed her, not saying anything but just watching her, until his intense gaze began to grate on her nerves even more badly than the approaching storm.

'Why don't you go back to the car?' she said edgily. 'It must be very boring for you, just watching me draw.'

'You've never bored me,' he said softly.

She started to say something, but then stopped. She had the feeling that it would be much safer to ignore that last remark.

Julius's gaze remained fixed on her and she could feel herself beginning to squirm inside. Why was he doing this? she wondered crossly. What was this all about?

She finally had all the drawings she wanted. She closed up her sketchbook and shoved it back into her bag. 'That's it,' she said with some relief. 'We can go back to the house now.'

Julius looked at her rather intently. 'This morning you couldn't wait to leave the house. Now you sound as if you can't wait to get back there.' His eyes began to glow again. 'Why, Jessamy? Do you feel safer there?'

She scowled at him. 'No, I don't feel safe there. And I *don't* want to be there. The only place I really want to be is my own flat.'

'Do you really hate it at my house so much?'

'No, I don't hate it,' she admitted at last, in a low mutter. 'The house is too beautiful, no one could really hate living there, even if it *is* much too quiet. But it isn't home.'

'It's my home. At least, I want it to be. But that's the real problem, isn't it, Jessamy? You don't like living under my roof.'

She swung round to face him. 'Of course it's the problem,' she said with sudden fierceness. 'And since you know it, I don't understand why you're making me stay there. What's the point of it, Julius?'

'The point is that I want to be near you.'

Her blue eyes opened wider. 'Why? Four years we've been apart, and you've never once tried to get in touch with me. On the couple of occasions that we accidentally met, you looked as if you actually wanted to hit me!'

'No one likes coming face to face with their mistakes,' he growled.

'And that's what I was?' she flashed back at him angrily. 'A mistake?'

Julius's face darkened. 'You know very well what I mean.'

'Oh, yes, I know!' Jessamy retorted. 'And our marriage definitely *was* a mistake. But it's one that I've already decided to put right. I want a divorce, Julius. This separation has gone on for far too long. It's holding both of us back; we're not getting on with our lives in the way that we should.'

He looked absolutely thunderous now. Jessamy flinched, but told herself she wasn't frightened. She wasn't going to let him intimidate her any more.

'I won't agree to a divorce,' he warned, and moved closer, as if trying to intimidate her physically with the powerful bulk of his body.

'You don't have to,' she said defiantly. 'Very soon I'll be able to get one on the grounds of separation.'

'We're not living apart at the moment,' he reminded her.

'We're certainly not living together!'

'You might have some difficulty convincing a judge of that. After all, we have spent these last few days in a very secluded country house. The kind of place that the gutter press likes to describe as a love nest.'

Jessamy stared at him for a moment, then her mouth set into a line that was almost as determined as his own. 'No, you're not getting away with that. I'll explain the circumstances exactly, and I'll make very sure that everyone believes me. Anyway, why won't you agree to a divorce?' she challenged him. 'You don't want me and you don't need me. You must have other women in your life. You've certainly had them in the past,' she reminded him, ignoring the small, unexpected twist of pain inside her as she said the words. 'The gossip columnists could hardly keep track of them! You must have worn yourself out, trying to satisfy all of them!'

'You don't know what you're talking about,' said Julius, and this time a warning note of a very different kind sounded in his voice.

'Did the newspapers invent those women?' she enquired sarcastically. 'Did they make up all those pictures of blondes, brunettes, redheads, hanging on to your arm?'

The dark stormclouds overhead were nothing compared to the ominous light now shining in Julius's eyes.

'I attended various social functions that required me to have a female escort,' he said through clenched teeth.

'And of course you didn't take any of them home afterwards,' she deliberately taunted him.

'No, I didn't!' he roared at her.

Jessamy involuntarily backed away. Julius in this mood was an intimidating sight! She wasn't ready to abandon the argument, though. 'I don't believe you,' she said flatly.

'Why should you?' he said savagely. 'You never knew how messed up I became after we broke up. Do you know why I never took any of those women home, Jessamy? Because I didn't want them. I couldn't even pretend that I wanted them! If I couldn't have you, then I didn't want anyone. You left me virtually impotent!'

Jessamy stared at him in numb shock. She tried to swallow, but couldn't, her throat had almost closed up.

'I—I——' She realised she was trying to say she was sorry. Then she stopped. The words were too futile and inadequate. She took a very long and deep breath.

Then she said in a small, flat voice, 'If you've got problems, then there are professional people who can probably help you. You're not going to mess up my life a second time, though, Julius. It's taken me four years to get to the point where I can live without you, start to look forward to the future, and you're *not* going to take that away from me. I want you to leave me alone!'

She hadn't known she could be so hard. It was a matter of self-survival, though. Julius had nearly destroyed her once. She dared not let it happen again.

She turned away from him and began to walk blindly back to the car. Lightning cracked overhead and she wished fervently that the storm would break and the rain begin to fall, washing away the sudden betraying wetness on her cheeks.

CHAPTER SEVEN

THEY drove back to the house in absolute silence. The storm which had threatened slowly rolled away again, the heavy clouds retreating to a grey line on the horizon and the thunder rumbling only softly in the distance. The air remained unnaturally hot and humid for the time of the year, and the sun shone down again from the brightening sky.

Jessamy's mood didn't reflect the change in the weather. She felt as if she were still surrounded by ominous shadows that no amount of sunlight would ever be able to penetrate.

Beside her, Julius's dark gaze remained fixed on the road ahead. He didn't once look at her; he behaved as if she weren't even there.

When they arrived at the house, Jessamy grabbed hold of her bag, went straight into the house and headed for the drawing-room.

'Work,' she told herself feverishly, tipping her sketches out on to the table. 'That's what you've got to do. *Work*. Get involved with the illustrations and forget about everything else.'

Only it was so hard to do that, especially when she began looking at the sketches she had made at-Kenilworth. Her pencil had captured the dark, brooding atmosphere only too well. Julius featured in none of the drawings, but she still seemed to see him; she could see that sudden haunted look in his eyes.

She pushed the sketches of Kenilworth away from

her with an abrupt movement. Try working on the drawings of Warwick, she told herself. Warwick was safer. Nothing too disturbing had happened at Warwick.

Except that she could still see Julius in every drawing. In the end, she threw her pencil across the room in frustration, then paced over to the window.

Outside, the garden looked more beautiful than ever in the golden light of late afternoon. The flowers bloomed happily in the soft sunshine, complemented by the gently swaying leaves of the trees, which were just beginning to be touched by the colours of autumn.

Jessamy found herself resenting the tranquillity of the scene when she felt so very unpeaceful inside herself. Damn Julius! she muttered to herself in a great surge of resentment. What right did he have to come back into her life like this, trying to shatter it into little pieces that couldn't be put back together for a second time?

The rest of the day passed by with appalling slowness. She couldn't eat, couldn't concentrate on her work, couldn't do anything except wander round and round the drawing-room, frightened to set foot outside the door in case she bumped straight into Julius.

Late in the evening, she finally slipped up to her bedroom, walking barefooted so that she wouldn't be heard. Once inside, she bolted the door and at last allowed herself to relax a little. For a few hours, at least, she would be safe. Not even Julius would be able to break his way through that very solid door.

After tossing restlessly for half the night, she managed to get a couple of hours' sleep, and woke up in the morning feeling very angry with herself. Why was she behaving like this? It was ridiculous, letting herself get worked up into this state. It was Julius who was having problems, not her. Well, let him deal with them himself! They were absolutely nothing to do with her. She didn't even have to think about them.

She took an almost cold shower, then pulled on a clean pair of jeans and found a T-shirt that didn't have too many paint stains on it. She clipped the long, dark swathes of her hair back from her face with a couple of combs; then she slowly walked over and looked at herself in the mirror.

A familiar reflection stared back at her. A girl who looked younger than her twenty-four years, lightly tanned and healthy, although the faint marks caused by a string of sleepless nights were beginning to appear around her eyes. Jessamy sighed. What had Julius seen in the nineteen-year-old girl she had been five years ago that had made him want to grab her and marry her, without even really knowing her? She knew it had been against his better judgement; that all his own instincts had told him to wait, to take it more slowly. Something had sparked into life when they had first set eyes on each other, though, and even Julius's self-control had melted away as the spark had ignited a flame, and then a fire.

Jessamy had been as overwhelmed as he had been, dazzled by the physical passion, and amazed that her own easygoing, relaxed attitude to life could be turned upside down by this one man. She had trusted him completely; had given in at once when he had demanded that they get married immediately.

The first few months had been sheer bliss. Then there had been the months of creeping doubt, the lack of any real communication between them, and the hostile silences when Julius had refused even to admit that anything was wrong. Finally, there had been the last few months, when everything had fallen apart with such shattering swiftness. Even in bed, sweet pleasure had turned to disaster. The harder Julius had tried, the less she had seemed able to respond to him, she had just frozen up inside. And once the sex had gone, there had really been nothing left at all.

Jessamy closed her eyes. Don't think about it! she instructed herself a little wildly. You've only been able to get through the last four years by not thinking about it.

With a huge effort, she managed to get everything back under control again. The old memories were stuffed back into the dark, locked cupboard at the very back of her mind, where she kept them safely shut away. Then she forced a carefully neutral expression on to her face, took a couple of very deep, steadying breaths, and left the bedroom.

The house seemed silent and deserted. No sign of Julius; in fact, no sign of life at all.

She went down to the kitchen and cooked herself a large breakfast. She couldn't remember when she had last eaten and, although she still wasn't hungry, she made herself swallow every mouthful.

She was just drinking a second cup of coffee when Julius walked through the doorway. The food she had eaten immediately seemed to stick inside her like a great lump of lead. She swallowed hard and then looked up at him.

His face was quite unreadable. Jessamy remembered all the times she had seen him look like that in the past, when he hadn't wanted her to know what he was thinking or feeling. She had always hated it; it made her feel so shut out. But then there was nothing new about feeling like that, she reminded herself grimly. It had been one of the reasons their marriage had failed.

When Julius finally spoke, his voice was as unemotional as his face.

'You probably don't want to see me this morning, but I've a good reason for being here. I want to apologise.'

Jessamy stared at him. 'Apologise?' she echoed at last.

He paced rather restlessly over to the far side of the kitchen. 'Yesterday wasn't a good day for either of us. I never intended it to turn out like that. I wanted us to spend a few hours together, just talking and relaxing.'

'So why did it go wrong?' she asked a little bitterly.

His shoulders lifted in a resigned shrug. 'I don't know.'

'That's always the problem, isn't it?' Her voice merely sounded tired now. 'We never seem to know why things don't work between us.'

'Do you think we could try again?' Then he smiled thinly as he saw the look on her face. 'Don't look so shocked, I'm not suggesting we try and revive whatever kind of relationship we once had. Credit me with some intelligence, Jessamy. I know that would never work.'

'Then what *are* you suggesting?' she asked warily.

'Only that we try and spend some time together again. And this time I want us both to make an effort to keep things friendly and pleasant. You won't be staying here for very much longer, and I don't want your last memory of me to be the way I was yesterday.'

But Jessamy didn't think she could cope with spending even half an hour with Julius.

'I don't think that would be a good idea,' she muttered. 'It wouldn't achieve anything.'

'I think it could achieve a great deal,' replied Julius. 'You said yesterday that you wanted a divorce, so that you could start a new life.'

'And you said you wouldn't agree,' she reminded him sharply.

'Yes, I did. But I'm beginning to see that there isn't much point in trying to hold on to something that doesn't belong to me. That's never really belonged to me.' He gave a dry smile. 'You know us Taureans— we only fight when we know we can win. I can't force you to want me. But I do want a chance to convince you that you don't have to hate me. And if you're determined to make a new life for yourself, Jessamy, it would be much better for you if you didn't end the old one on a sour note. It'll only make things that much harder for you. Why not try to leave here with at least a few pleasant memories?'

She was silent for quite a long time. What Julius had said made a lot of sense. It *would* make things a lot easier for her—for both of them—if they could manage to end this marriage on a fairly amicable note, instead of in a flood of tension and arguments.

'I really ought to get on with some work,' she said at last, waveringly. 'I've got a deadline to meet.'

'Bring your drawing materials with you. We'll go somewhere that you can use in your illustrations.'

'We tried that yesterday—and it didn't work!' she reminded him, her eyes briefly flaring.

'Today won't be like yesterday,' Julius promised, his own dark gaze resting on her steadily.

Jessamy gave a small sigh. Would it be totally insane of her to agree to his suggestion? But part of her *did* want to repair some of the damage they had done to each other. And perhaps Julius was right. If they could learn to be civil to each other, maybe even friendly, it would make it very much easier to walk away from him when this was all over.

'All right,' she said slowly, after another very long pause. 'We'll try spending a couple of hours together. But if it starts to go wrong again, I'm walking out,' she warned him.

Part of her had the feeling that she was making a very big mistake. The decision had been made now, though. She would go with Julius—and by the time they returned to the house she would know if they were going to part as friends or enemies.

She went slowly back to the drawing-room to collect her sketch-pad and pencils, and all the time she kept telling herself that this was a really stupid thing to do. Change your mind right now, she advised herself. Only an absolute idiot would risk a repeat of yesterday.

But Jessamy still kept going, picking up her drawing materials and then walking out to the car. This is crazy, she told herself for the umpteenth time. Then Julius got into the car beside her and started up the engine, and it was too late to get out.

'Where are we going?' she asked, as the car moved smoothly down the road and then on through the small village just beyond.

'Not very far,' he said. 'In fact, if I do or say anything that you really object to, you'll be able to walk back to the house.'

Jessamy wasn't sure if that made her feel better or not. 'But you're not going to do or say anything objectionable, are you?' she said pointedly.

Julius gave an odd smile. 'I'll try not to. But I don't always seem to be fully in control of myself when you're around.'

She wasn't at all sure she liked the sound of that. She was about to say so, in no uncertain terms, but stopped herself at the last moment. This might be one of those times when it was far better to say nothing!

The car purred smoothly on along a narrow lane lined with trees. A short distance further on, Julius turned off on to what was little more than a narrow track.

He parked the car in the shade of a nearby tree, then cut the engine.

'We'll have to walk from here,' he told her.

'Walk where?' she asked suspiciously.

'You'll see when we get there. It isn't far.'

Jessamy got out of the car, then trudged after him as he strode easily along the track. It began to climb fairly steeply upwards, and she started to get rather out of breath.

'I thought you said it wasn't far,' she grumbled.

'Another couple of minutes, and we'll be there.'

The track wound past one last stand of trees, then petered out as it reached a wide, open space at the top of the hill. Jessamy puffed her way to the end of the track, then stood still, partly because she needed to get her breath back and partly because she was startled by the sight in front of her.

A circle of standing stones ringed the open space, ancient and mysterious. Some stood upright, while others leaned rather drunkenly. Tall grass swayed around them in the gentle breeze, and the sun reflected dully off the stones' pitted surfaces.

Julius turned and gave her a faint smile. 'Not quite as spectacular as Stonehenge, but I thought you might find them interesting.'

Jessamy slowly walked forward and rubbed her hand gently over the rough surface of the nearest stone.

'Why are they here?' she asked at last.

'No one knows for certain, although plenty of theories have been put forward. Some people think they're connected with religious ceremonies, others that they have some kind of astronomical significance. No one even knows how long they've been here. A thousand years, two thousand—your guess is as good as anyone's.'

She moved to the centre of the ring. From here she could see the folds of the surrounding hills and valleys, basking in the warm autumn sunshine.

'This place has a really eerie atmosphere,' she said in a hushed voice. 'I wouldn't want to come here at night!'

Julius walked forward until he was standing only a few feet away. 'This place suits you,' he said, looking at her.

She pulled a face. 'You mean I look prehistoric?'

'No. Just that the circle seems rather mysterious, and that's how you seem to me a lot of the time.'

'There's nothing mysterious about me,' Jessamy said firmly. 'I'm very down-to-earth and practical.'

At that, Julius's eyebrows shot up. 'You draw pictures that are pure fantasy,' he reminded her. 'You have problems handling money, and you can't drive a car. And if I remember rightly, you're not too good at using even simple electrical gadgets.'

'I am practical,' Jessamy insisted with some annoyance. 'My money problems are only temporary, I'd learn to drive if I only had time for the lessons, and you'd be surprised at how many gadgets I've learned to use and even repair during the past four years. Don't make me sound like an idiot, Julius!'

'I never meant to do any such thing,' he told her softly. 'And if you like, I'll list all your good points. You're beautiful to look at, you're full of charm and innocence, and when you smile—I wish you'd smile more often—it's like a bright ray of sunshine on a dark day. You like to argue, but you're never overbearing. Next to you, I often feel clumsy and domineering. You thought I was criticising you, but I certainly wasn't. I like you exactly the way you are.'

Jessamy was so shaken by his quietly spoken reply that she couldn't stop herself from over-reacting.

'Oh, sure!' she retorted. 'You liked me so much that you walked out on me!' Her blue eyes were overbright, and she immediately regretted that those words had burst out of her. Rather abruptly, she turned away from him. 'I don't want to go over all that again,' she muttered in a much more subdued tone. 'Let's try and forget I said it. I don't think I want to stay here, though. Let's go back to the house.'

'But we've only just got here,' said Julius, in a surprisingly reasonable tone of voice.

'I know, but this isn't working out. I shouldn't have come. We can't seem to spend any time together without getting involved in all the old arguments again.'

'You're the one who seems to be starting this particular argument,' he pointed out levelly.

She gave a tired shrug. 'Does it matter who starts it? It always ends the same. You'll clam up or walk away as soon as it gets to be too personal.'

'I'm not going anywhere, at the moment.'

'But you will, if this goes on for much longer. I'll end up talking to a blank space—as usual!'

'I'm not going anywhere,' Julius repeated, in a very even voice. 'I promise. Now, do you want to get on with your sketches? I don't want to be blamed for making you miss your deadline, as well as for everything else.'

Jessamy began to say something, but then stopped. She had enough sense to realise that this was one argument that ought to come to a stop right now.

'I'll just do a few sketches,' she muttered. 'Then we can go back to the car.'

As she opened her drawing-pad, Julius settled himself on the grass, his back propped up against one of the stones. He closed his eyes, as if he were tired, and Jessamy found that her gaze kept straying to him, instead of concentrating on the blank sheet in front of her.

His face was so familiar. She knew she could close her eyes and still remember every line with perfect clarity. She also knew why she had come here with him today. It was quite simply that she had wanted to be with him. And that was very scary, because it was so much safer not to want anything at all, where Julius was concerned.

She forced herself to look away from him. Her fingers began to move over the sheet of paper, but when she had finished drawing the circle of standing stones, she found she had also sketched in the figure of Julius.

'Stop it!' she told herself out loud.

Julius's eyes opened. 'Did you say something?' he asked.

'No,' she said hurriedly. 'At least, not to you. I was talking to myself.'

'Come and sit down here, and talk to me instead,'
he invited.

Jessamy swallowed hard. 'I—I don't think we have
anything to discuss,' she got out rather stiffly.

A flicker of amusement showed in his dark eyes. 'We
don't have to talk about anything personal, if that will
make you feel any safer.'

'I feel perfectly safe,' she said very firmly, and hoped
he couldn't tell that was an outright lie.

'Then there's no reason why you shouldn't come and
sit with me for a few minutes. We don't have to say
anything at all, if talking makes you nervous. We'll
relax in the sunshine for a while, then we'll walk back
to the car.'

Even though his suggestion sounded absolutely
harmless, Jessamy still didn't want to go along with it.
If she insisted on going straight back to the car, though,
it would look as if she was running away. She didn't
want to do that either. It would be tantamount to
admitting that being close to him made her nervous,
and nothing was going to make her do that. She was
determined not to let him know he still had the power
to make her feel anything at all.

She sat down rather stiffly on the grass, being careful
to keep a safe distance between them. Julius briefly
looked amused again but, to her relief, he didn't say
anything.

The sun blazed down on the ancient circle of stones,
bees buzzed diligently as they searched for late pollen,
and birds sang cheerfully in the nearby trees.

'This weather is freakish,' Jessamy said a couple of
minutes later, shading her eyes against the bright blaze
of the sun.

'Make the most of it,' he advised. 'I doubt if it's

going to last much longer. By next week there could be dull skies, rain and cold winds.'

She settled back more comfortably on the grass. 'I don't even want to think about next week,' she said, stifling a yawn.

'I thought you'd be looking forward to it. By that time we should have sorted out this business of the poison pen letter and you'll be able to get back to a normal life again.'

'I've almost forgotten what it's like to live a normal life,' she said drily. Then she yawned again. All those nights when she hadn't been able to sleep seemed to be catching up with her. She was finding it hard to keep her eyes open.

Don't go to sleep, she told herself dozily. People always look so vulnerable when they're asleep. Her eyes kept flickering shut, though, and they finally stayed closed as she gently snoozed.

When she woke up again, for a couple of seconds she couldn't remember where she was. Warm sunshine, soft grass, and the clear scent of fresh air—she definitely wasn't in bed!

Then she squinted upwards, and saw Julius looking down at her. An instant later she remembered exactly where she was. And almost immediately after that she realised that Julius had moved much closer.

She hurriedly sat up and glared edgily at him. 'Have you been watching me while I've been asleep?' she demanded accusingly.

'I always liked to watch you sleep,' Julius said in a soft voice. 'It made me feel as if everything was all right with the world. You always looked so relaxed, so untroubled.'

'Well, there were times when I definitely didn't *feel* untroubled,' she retorted.

His face began to change, and small, shadowed lines appeared at the corners of his mouth and eyes.

'And that was all my fault, of course,' he said in a rather tight voice. 'My God, Jessamy, do you blame me for absolutely everything that went wrong between us?'

'No,' she said at last, after a very long pause. 'Some of it had to be my fault. I was too young, I didn't know how to handle things—didn't know how to handle *you*. And there were so many new pressures—the long hours you worked, the way your parents disapproved of me, the problems I was having trying to get my own career off the ground. It was so hard to cope with all of them. And I couldn't even talk to you about them. When you were home—which didn't seem to be very often!—you didn't want to listen. You were so stubborn about it, you just kept saying everything was all right, and it wasn't, it was getting worse all the time, and I couldn't understand why you couldn't see it. Then I finally realised you could see it, but you'd decided simply to ignore it. I suppose you thought everything would somehow miraculously work itself out. And once you'd made your decision, you dug your feet in and *nothing* would make you change your mind. There was just no way I could get you to talk to me. I still don't know how to do it,' she said in a suddenly tired voice. 'I've never been able to get through to you, Julius.'

'You got through to me only too well! You took me apart so thoroughly that, even now, I can't put the pieces back together again.'

Jessamy stared at him in utter disbelief. '*I* took *you*

apart?' she said incredulously. 'I was nineteen years old, and pretty naïve for my age. I didn't know how to take anyone apart!'

'Whether you knew how to or not, you did it.' His dark eyes abruptly bored into her. 'Are you sure you didn't do it on purpose? To prove that you had some sort of power over me?'

That took her breath away. 'Do you really think I wanted to go through all that?' she demanded fiercely. 'Do you have any idea what it did to me?'

'Oh, yes, I know,' he said in a low voice. 'Because it did exactly the same thing to me.'

Her blue eyes flared very brightly. 'I don't believe that! You were so much older than me, you'd been through broken relationships before and knew how to cope with them. For me, it was the very first time. I didn't know what the hell was happening, and I certainly didn't know how to cope with it!'

Julius's own eyes grew stormy. 'A broken relationship isn't anything like a broken marriage. Yes, there had been women in my life before I met you — very few men in their thirties have lived like a monk. Those relationships were based on affection, though. That was all I ever felt for any woman—until I met you.' A note of bitter sarcasm entered his voice. 'Don't you know that you caught me at an age when Taureans are at their most vulnerable? It's when they're most likely to fall in love, once and for ever. It was just that I never expected it to happen to *me*.'

'I wish it hadn't!' she said with equal bitterness. 'Or that you'd at least had some control over what happened.'

'What are you telling me? That I shouldn't have swept you straight off to the church? But I knew that almost from the very start,' he said grimly. 'You were too immature, the age difference between us was too great. I knew I should wait for you to grow up. I ignored all my instincts—and paid for it.'

Jessamy threw a contemptuous look at him. 'Are you going to pretend that the age difference was our only problem? Aren't you forgetting that we also had a serious communication problem? Or rather, you did! The only place I seemed to be able to reach you was in bed. You never wanted to discuss your work, you wouldn't talk to me about any personal problems; sometimes I used to think that there wasn't one single damned thing we *could* talk about.'

'It's the way I am,' Julius said grimly. 'I thought you understood that. You'd met my father and mother, you knew I'd been raised in a very repressed, almost Victorian household. Voices were never raised, controversial issues were never discussed, conversation was confined to polite remarks about the weather and social events. Since childhood, I'd been taught to keep everything to myself—problems, opinions, feelings. I couldn't break free of the habit even after I reached adulthood. And I wasn't sure I even wanted to. It fitted in with my own nature.'

'I just felt shut out all the time,' Jessamy said dully. 'Except when we were making love—that was the only time you seemed to let me anywhere near you.'

'That was the way I tried to show you that I loved you,' Julius answered in a low voice. 'I couldn't say it, but I wanted you to know it, and that was the only way I could try and tell you.'

'Well, it didn't work, did it?' she said rather tiredly. 'Or perhaps you just tried too hard. In the end, it seemed that sex was all you ever wanted from me. I couldn't cope with a relationship that was so physical, I started to freeze up when you touched me. I needed to share all your life, not just a few hours in bed every night.'

A dark shadow crossed Julius's face. 'I knew you were drifting away from me. I thought that in some way I wasn't pleasing you. I set out to put that right, but the harder I tried, the more I failed.'

She shook her head slowly. 'All that intense passion, the long hours in bed when you made love to me over and over, but never *said* anything—it just turned me off. We were lying there so close together, but there seemed to be a mile-wide gulf between us. And you kept trying all those complicated ways of pleasing me, but all I wanted was for you just to *want* me.'

'Dear God, do you think I didn't?' Julius said roughly.

'I know you did. But it was the wrong kind of wanting. It seemed to be so physical, and nothing else. I tried to tell you, but you wouldn't listen. I suppose it was because we would have had to talk about it then, and you'd already decided you weren't going to do that. Which brings us back to the old problem,' she finished on a slightly bitter note.

'We're talking now,' Julius said in a steadier tone.

'Yes, we are—when it's too late. Perhaps you've finally begun to change, Julius. What a pity you couldn't have talked to me four years ago, instead of simply walking out.'

'I didn't know what else to do,' he said in a low tone. 'All my life, I've been successful at everything I've done. In fact, I'd been brought up to regard failure at anything as the ultimate sin. And I finally had to admit that I was failing in my marriage to you. I'd even begun

to fail in bed. Everything was falling apart, and I didn't
know how to stop it. So in the end I turned my back
on it and walked away. At the time, it was the only
way I knew how to deal with it. I made the decision to
put my marriage behind me, forget about it, and start
over again. Only I couldn't do it. The last four years
have been a nightmare that wouldn't go away, no
matter what I did. I tried working myself into the
ground, but I could be totally exhausted and *still*
remember. I wanted to try other women, but I couldn't
bring myself to do it. For the first couple of years, I
was angry, permanently bad-tempered, and sexually
frustrated. Then the anger faded away and the desire
died with it. Everything went a terrible shade of grey
after that. I thought I was never going to want anything
ever again.'

His voice had become blank, as if reflecting the utter
bleakness of his life. Jessamy had almost stopped
breathing. She couldn't believe Julius was saying all
these things to her. Julius, who had always kept his
personal thoughts and feelings under lock and key.
Julius, who during their brief engagement and marriage
had never even told her he loved her.

They sat in silence for a very long time, surrounded
by the ancient circle of stones. Despite the heat of the
sun, her skin was crawling with goosepimples. Then
she actually shivered.

Julius immediately noticed her reaction. 'Perhaps it
wasn't a very good idea to talk about this, to drag it all
out into the open again.'

'I don't see how it can help, not after all this time,'
she agreed shakily. 'But right now, I can't think of
anything that *would* help.'

'How about this?' he suggested softly. Then he leant forward and very gently kissed her.

'No, Julius,' she muttered instinctively. They mustn't go down this road again, it could only lead to disaster.

But he was already kissing her again, more hungrily this time. She tried to draw back, but his hands came up and gripped her, refusing to let her go.

'No,' Jessamy said again, but her voice was more uncertain this time.

'I need to do this,' he said, his voice becoming more intense. His mouth closed over hers again, the touch of it as intoxicating as it had been the very first time he had kissed her. The sun shone down on them hotly, and the warmth seemed to confuse her wits, befuddle her brain. Or was it the heat of Julius's body that was having such an odd effect on her?

His hands slid under her thin T-shirt, but he made no effort to remove it. Instead his mouth pressed against the soft cotton, tracing the outline of her body and making her shudder.

Her own fingers touched the dark silkiness of his hair. The well-remembered texture of it triggered off vivid flashes of memory, so that past and present blurred together, confusing her still further. As if sensing it, Julius took advantage of it, pushing her lightly back on to the grass.

The weight of his body was very familiar. So was the hard, strong outline of his body, very evident even through the covering of his clothes. Jessamy couldn't stop herself from moving restlessly. How many times had he caused this quick, sudden ache in her? And known exactly how to satisfy it?

She blinked hard. Something was wrong, but it was almost impossible to remember what it was. And Julius was making it even more difficult, because the silken-smooth touch of his fingers was already producing mind-numbing waves of pleasure.

How frightening that it could happen again so easily. Jessamy was aware of that thought drifting into her head, but she couldn't hold on to it, and it drifted out again. Julius moved closer and she became aware that his skin was very hot. But so was hers. Fire meeting fire. The flames were already flickering just beneath the surface, waiting to be fanned into fierce, burning life. His tongue licked the small nerve-points that he could so easily locate, and she shivered even through the heat. Julius murmured softly in satisfaction and his body pressed still closer, demanding more now, desire a hard ache that was threatening to run out of control.

He bent his head to her breast again, still nuzzling through the thin cotton, as if finding a perverse pleasure in delaying the moment when his lips would trail their way across her flushed skin. The sun blazed down into her eyes, dazzling her, in the same way that Julius was dazzling her body into submission. The fire spread through her limbs, nerve-ends felt red-hot, and still the heat increased until she felt as if she might burn up completely.

At that moment she was totally vulnerable. If he had tried to tear the clothes from her, she probably wouldn't—couldn't—have stopped him. Instead, though, he lifted his head and looked down at her, his dark eyes bright and a faint flush of colour running along his cheekbones.

'I can't just take what I want,' he said thickly. 'Not any more. I don't have the right. But I'm asking you, Jessamy. Please, let me. Just this once——'

She stared up at him in astonishment. She hadn't

known that her decisive, forceful husband was capable of asking—begging—for something. Perhaps he hadn't been—until this moment.

But he had also given her time to think what she was doing. To realise what was happening. The sun suddenly seemed to lose a little of its warmth. She felt her own skin begin to feel chilled as the heat slowly ebbed away.

If she said yes, then it would be like taking a giant step backwards. Everything she had tried to achieve for herself during the last four years would have to be tossed away, useless. She would have to begin all over again, and she really didn't think she could do that. It had taken all her strength to get this far in her life. It would be madness to throw it all away for a few moments of nerve-storming passion.

'Julius——' she began, but she choked over his name. She closed her eyes so that she wouldn't have to look at him. 'I can't,' she said in a suddenly lifeless voice. 'I'm sorry, but I just can't.'

She felt the wave of shock that ran through him as her words hit him. Then the enormous effort that he had to make to move away from her, rolling heavily on to his back and then staring up at the sky.

Neither of them moved or spoke for several minutes. Then Julius got slowly to his feet, looking very much older than his thirty-six years.

'I suppose we'd better go back to the car,' he said in a carefully neutral tone.

Jessamy tried to say something, but then stopped. Words would only make the situation even worse—if that were possible.

They drove back to the house in silence. When the

car finally came to a halt, she looked straight ahead of her, not daring to look at him.

'I'll leave,' she said. 'I'll go straight away. I'll book into a hotel, and make sure that whoever sent that poison pen letter won't be able to find me.'

Julius gave an odd, twisted smile. 'And *I* won't be able to find you?'

'I can't stay here!' she burst out edgily.

'I know that.' She had the feeling that he was finding it extraordinarily difficult to keep his own voice even. 'I'll ring for a taxi,' he went on in a flat tone. He began to open the car door, but then stopped. 'It really is over, isn't it,' he said, and it was a statement, not a question.

'Yes, it's over,' she said dully.

They got out of the car and headed towards the house. And although they walked side by side, Jessamy felt as if there were an invisible, impenetrable wall between them.

CHAPTER EIGHT

WHEN they reached the house, Julius opened the door and they went inside.

'I'll go straight up and pack,' Jessamy said in a subdued voice. Julius didn't even reply. She had the feeling that he had run completely out of words.

She went up the stairs on legs that felt absolutely leaden. She was so preoccupied with what had happened that she wasn't taking any notice of anything as she opened the door and went into her room. Then she gradually became aware that something was very wrong.

Her clothes were spread out all over the bed, and at first she couldn't figure out what they were doing there. Then her eyes slowly began to focus and she realised that they hadn't just been tossed on to the bed. They had been slashed.

Jessamy's skin went cold. She took another step forward, and saw the few personal items she had brought with her lying on the floor. They were smashed to pieces, as if someone had ground them underfoot.

Not one single thing she had brought with her had been left untouched. Drawers and cupboards had been completely emptied, and everything had been broken, ripped and destroyed.

She began to shake. Who could hate her enough to do such a thing? And how had they found her *here*? Julius had told her that hardly anyone knew he owned this house.

She looked around nervously as another thought occurred to her. What if whoever had done this was still inside the house? If they had done this to her possessions, what would they do if they actually came face to face with her?

On trembling legs, she retreated towards the door. It was terrifying to think that someone could feel such hatred towards you that they could do something like this. All that destructive force—and all of it directed towards her.

She suddenly knew she had to get out of the house. Rather blindly, she began to grope her way towards the stairs. She couldn't think of anything except getting away from here; away from that room with all her destroyed belongings.

She reached the stairs, and stumbled down them. On top of everything else that had happened today, this was just too much. She couldn't cope with it; couldn't seem to cope with *anything* any more.

When she reached the bottom of the stairs, she began to run towards the door. She was almost there when a strong arm suddenly shot out and stopped her.

Jessamy screamed. Then she almost collapsed with relief when she heard Julius's voice.

'What the hell's going on?' he demanded.

'Up—upstairs——' she stammered rather incoherently. 'Someone's been—been in my room. They've—they've——' She couldn't seem to finish what she was trying to say.

Julius's dark eyes bored into her, as if trying to work out what was going on. 'Wait here,' he instructed at last. 'I'll take a look.'

As soon as he let go of her, she began to edge

towards the door. His hand immediately gripped her again.

'Stay here,' he ordered again. 'I don't want you to go anywhere until I get back. Promise me, Jessamy.'

She looked longingly towards the door. Outside, she would feel safe. There would be fresh air and golden evening sunlight and freedom. She knew better than to disobey Julius when he used that particular tone of voice, though.

'I promise,' she muttered.

He went quickly upstairs after that, leaving her to stand there, still gently shaking. He was back in just a couple of minutes, and his face was set into dark, angry lines.

'You saw?' she said.

'Yes, I saw,' he confirmed in a tight voice.

'I'm not safe here any more, am I?' she said in a quavering tone. 'Whoever wrote that poison pen letter has found me. They've destroyed all my things—and I think they want to destroy me.'

'As long as you're with me, you'll be safe.'

'How can you say that?' she demanded edgily. 'I want to get out of here, get right away from this house, before they come back again. I'm scared,' she admitted, with a shiver.

He immediately took hold of her hands in a warm, firm grip.

'There's no need to be. No one's going to harm you.'

'You don't know that! Until you find the person who sent that letter, I'm *never* going to be completely safe.'

Julius looked at her levelly. 'I already know who sent that letter.'

That sent a sharp jolt of shock through her. She

raised her head and stared at him, her blue eyes very wide.

'You know? Who was it? Tell me!'

'It was Eleanor,' he said quietly.

'*Eleanor*?' There was clear disbelief in her tone. 'I know she dislikes me, but. . .Eleanor,' she said again, as she began to realise that it made a lot of sense. 'Are you absolutely sure?' she asked, still not totally convinced.

'She left a copy of that poison pen letter she sent you on her word-processor,' Julius said. 'She probably meant to erase it, but forgot. Quite by chance, I saw it.'

Jessamy's gaze began to harden. 'Then you knew all along that it was her,' she said accusingly. 'You could have told me that at the very beginning, and put a stop to the whole thing right then. There was no need for you to bring me here, no need to keep me here.'

'Yes, there was,' he said levelly. '*I* wanted you here. Eleanor simply gave me the excuse I needed. I used her. I even brought her here so that I could see your reaction to her, see if that spark of jealousy you'd once felt towards her was still there.'

'I don't believe I'm hearing any of this,' Jessamy said angrily, shaking her head. 'You're as bad as she is, in a lot of ways!'

'I'm not particularly proud of the way I behaved. But I'd already decided that I had to see you again, spend some time with you, and this was one way of doing it.'

And she knew only too well how stubborn Julius could be once he had got an idea inside his head. If he had made up his mind to see her again, then he would have moved heaven and earth to accomplish it.

'I've had enough of this,' she muttered at last. 'You've *all* been playing games with me.'

'I'm not playing,' he told her steadily.

She refused to look at him. She had the feeling that, if she stared into those dark eyes, she might lose what little self-control she had left.

'What are you going to do about Eleanor?' she challenged him.

'Probably what I should have done in the first place. Hand the matter over to the police.' He gave a sudden frown. 'I never thought she'd go this far. She's always seemed so efficient, so controlled.'

'Eleanor's in love with you,' Jessamy reminded him impatiently. 'I told you that, but you wouldn't listen.'

'I didn't listen because I wasn't interested.' His tone changed and became a little thicker. 'I've only ever been interested in one woman.'

But Jessamy didn't want to hear that, not right now. She began to edge towards the door again.

'I've had enough of all this. I want to get out of here.'

'It's getting late. Stay here tonight, and leave in the morning.'

'No!' she said with sudden vehemence. 'I don't want to stay in this house one minute longer. Can't you understand that?'

'I realise you don't want to go back to your room again. But there are plenty of other rooms you can use. Rooms that Eleanor's never been near.'

'She's contaminated the whole house! I keep on thinking that I can even smell her perfume. And you say there are rooms she hasn't been in, but how do you *know*? She could have crept into any of them while she was here,' Jessamy said rather wildly, knowing she was being unreasonable, but quite unable to do anything about it. She was close to cracking up now, these final revelations had been just too much for her, she couldn't cope with them, not on top of everything else that had happened today. She held out her hand. 'Give me your keys. I'll spend the night in the car.'

'You can't sleep in the car.'

'I can do anything I damned well like!' she shouted back at him. Then, to her intense humiliation, she began to cry.

Julius at once put his arms round her. 'Let go of me,' she snuffled, but he took absolutely no notice. Instead, he waited until the first fierce flood of tears had passed, then loosened his grip on her a little. He didn't let go of her completely, though.

'I'd take you back to London, but I don't think you're in any fit state to go anywhere tonight,' he said. 'You need to rest for a while.'

'I'm not going to sleep in this house,' she insisted in a tearful, hiccupy voice.

'There are a couple of rooms over the stables,' he told her. 'They used to be the groom's flat. They'll probably be rather dusty, but they're quite separate from the house and I can guarantee that Eleanor's never set foot in them. How do you feel about staying there for the night? And in the morning I'll drive you back to your own flat.'

'Well—I don't know——' she mumbled. 'Have you got a hanky?' After he had handed her one, she blew her nose and scrubbed her eyes dry. She realised that she felt absolutely drained. She wanted to curl up in a small ball somewhere quiet, dark and safe, and stay there until she felt capable of facing the world again.

'You're sure Eleanor's never been near the stables?' she asked at last, in a small voice.

'Absolutely certain.'

'Then I suppose I could stay there. Just for tonight.'

'I'll take you over there now, then, and you can get settled in before it gets dark.'

She shuffled after him as he left the house, almost too exhausted now to put one foot in front of the other. It was quite a long walk to the stables, which were at the back of the house. When they got there, they went up an outside flight of stairs, then Julius took a bunch of keys out of his pocket.

'I haven't been in here since the day I first arrived at the house. It's probably in a fairly rough state.'

'I don't care,' she said. 'Just as long as it's got a bed.'

Julius got the door open, and she followed him inside. As he had said, it was just a couple of rooms, very simply furnished. A thin layer of dust covered everything, but Jessamy didn't care. She just wanted to collapse on to the bed she had spotted in the corner and sleep for about a week.

'The electricity isn't on, but there's running water,' he told her. 'I'll go back to the house and find you some clean sheets and blankets.'

When he had gone, Jessamy wandered into the small bedroom and sat down on the bed, because her legs felt as if they just wouldn't hold her up any longer. She still couldn't quite believe it was Eleanor who had sent her that poisonous letter, Eleanor who had destroyed her clothes and personal belongings. And Julius had known all along that it was Eleanor! She didn't think she would ever be able to forgive him for keeping that information from her.

Julius returned several minutes later, with an armful

of blankets. The light was beginning to fade now. Although the days were still warm and sunny, the evenings closed in early and the temperature soon began to dip as darkness approached. There was already a distinct chill in the air, and the rooms over the stables weren't heated.

As Julius came in, he noticed her shiver. 'Cold?' he queried, with a small frown. 'Here, put one of these blankets round you straight away.'

He tucked it around her shoulders. Then he sat down on the bed beside her.

'I'm all right now,' Jessamy said with sudden wariness. 'You don't have to stay any longer.'

'Yes, I do,' he said calmly. 'You're not just shivering from the cold. It's from shock as well. You need someone with you for a while.'

'No, I don't,' she insisted, but somehow there wasn't very much conviction in her voice. Not that it would have mattered if there had been, she told herself with resignation. Julius still wouldn't have taken any notice.

She shivered again, and he moved closer. She could feel his body against hers now, warm and familiar. She told herself she ought to edge away, but she couldn't make herself do it. Just for a few minutes, she needed to be near to him.

'Will Eleanor come back again?' she asked at last. 'Do you think she'll try something else?'

'If she does, she'll be very sorry,' he said in a grim tone. 'I can't understand why she's suddenly begun to behave like this. She must have had some kind of brainstorm.'

'Not a brainstorm,' Jessamy said drily. 'It's called love.'

'But you keep telling me she's been in love with me for years. Why hasn't she done this before?'

Jessamy had been thinking about it while she had been waiting for Julius to return with the blankets, and she thought she knew the answer.

'Because after you walked out on our marriage, she had you all to herself,' she said. 'That was important to her, I suppose she could convince herself that you belonged to her.'

'But she was just my secretary,' Julius said with a frown.

'I know, but she told me once that that was enough for her. It meant that she could see you every day, work closely with you, even travel abroad with you.' Jessamy managed a wry smile. 'They say a secretary spends as much time with her boss as his wife, perhaps even more. But you didn't even have a wife—at least, not one that you had any contact with. That must have made her feel as if you belonged to her exclusively. But then there was that newspaper review which mentioned that I was your wife, and Eleanor began to hear rumours about us getting back together again. I suppose she just couldn't stand the thought of having to share you. It made her go a little crazy.'

'Next time I pick a secretary, I'll be more careful,' growled Julius. 'I'll choose one who's middle-aged and matronly.'

'She'll probably still fall in love with you,' Jessamy said drily. Then she gave a small sigh. 'So much for my plans for running away from you. That's one more thing that Eleanor's messed up.'

'Would you have gone, if she hadn't destroyed your things?' Julius asked, his eyes glowing intently in the gathering darkness.

'Yes,' she admitted.

'Why?'

'Because—well, I suppose because being near you was beginning to make me very nervous.'

He looked a little incredulous. '*I* make you nervous?'

'It reminds me of things that I need to forget,' she said defensively. 'Nothing's really changed, Julius. Just because I'm staying here tonight, it doesn't mean—I don't want you to think—you mustn't assume——'

'I'm not assuming anything,' he said, and his own voice was surprisingly unruffled. 'Over the last four years I've had to learn to take each day—and night—as it comes. I'm not looking ahead or making any wild plans for the future.'

But Jessamy wasn't at all sure she believed him. She was sure Julius *did* have plans. That he had begun to make them when he had first discovered that letter on Eleanor's word-processor, and was following them with absolutely dogged determination.

'Do you think Eleanor's still around here somewhere?' she asked, in a hurry to change the subject. 'Perhaps she's staying locally?'

'Stop talking about Eleanor,' ordered Julius. 'Stop even thinking about her.'

'How can I do that?' she said edgily.

'That's easy. Think of something else instead.'

'What else *is* there to think about?'

'How about this?' he suggested.

His kiss was light, almost friendly. It was unlike any kiss that she could remember him giving her before.

'This really isn't a good idea,' she said with a small gulp.

'Why not?'

'Because——' She was alarmed to find she couldn't

think of any good reason. 'It just isn't,' she muttered stubbornly, at last.

'Isn't it better than thinking about Eleanor?' Julius said persuasively.

'There are a lot of other things we can do to stop ourselves thinking about her! We don't have to——'

'Don't have to do this?' he murmured. Then he found her mouth again and gave her another of those butterfly-light kisses. 'But I like doing it,' he added softly.

And so did she! Jessamy gave another audible gulp. This wasn't the way that she wanted things to be, she told herself a little frantically. In fact, she had wanted to get away from Julius to *stop* something like this happening.

She sat very still, staring ahead of her into the gathering darkness. 'I think it would be better if we sat a little further apart,' she said at last in a slightly cracked tone.

'Better for whom?' Julius enquired softly. 'I certainly don't think it would be better for me.'

'Yes, it would,' she insisted nervously. 'If we stay so close, you'll just want to—want to——'

'Want to do this?' he cut in.

This time his kiss was a little more forceful, it lasted longer, and she felt the first light outbreak of heat on his skin.

'Julius——' she said warningly. At least, she had meant to warn him. Instead, though, she was horrified to hear a clear note of something very different in her voice.

He heard it as well. Heard it, and instantly took advantage of it.

His next kiss was very different from the ones that

had gone before—swift, fierce and possessive, as if he were claiming back something that had always belonged to him.

'No more games,' he said roughly, as he finally had to draw his mouth away to drag in a quick snatch of breath. 'This is something that has to happen, Jessamy.'

But there was a part of her that still wouldn't give in to him without a fight. She had struggled too hard for her independence and peace of mind to give it up so easily.

'It doesn't have to happen,' she said, her voice almost as stubborn as his could be at times. 'We're two adults, we're mature, we can make rational decisions about our lives.'

'I don't feel like an adult. It's ridiculous, but I feel like a teenager, all fumbling hands and no control.'

She blinked. Julius *never* fumbled. And most of the time they had been together, he had had far too much control.

He smiled ruefully in the semi-darkness. 'Don't you believe me, Jessamy? Why don't you try touching me? Then you'll find out for yourself what it's doing to me, just being this near to you.'

Tentatively, she let her fingertips graze against his skin. It was burning hot. He felt as if he were running a high fever.

She shook her head in dismay. 'Please—don't force me into this.'

'You don't need to be forced into anything,' he said softly. 'Your skin's on fire as well. It's always been like this between us, Jessamy.'

'But that's the trouble,' she suddenly flared at him.

'That's all there's ever been between us! It wasn't enough the first time, and it won't be enough now.'

'You're wrong.' He said it with absolute certainty. 'We've always had more than just this. Even this is special, though. The way I want you is different from the way I've ever wanted any other woman. It isn't some shallow need that goes away after an hour in bed with you. It goes so much deeper than that. I want you in dozens of different ways, and only a few of them have anything to do with actual physical desire.'

'But we tried living together,' Jessamy reminded him almost angrily. 'And it didn't work.'

'Perhaps neither of us tried hard enough.'

'*I* tried!'

'Then maybe most of the faults were on my side. But if we tried again——'

'Don't do this to me, Julius,' she cut in fiercely. 'Before I came here, I had my life all sorted out, I was happy—at least, as happy as I ever expected to be. After four awful years, I finally felt I was getting somewhere. I was managing to put our disastrous marriage behind me, and I was even getting to the stage where I could look forward to the future. Don't mess me up again, because I couldn't cope with it, I couldn't put myself back together a second time!'

'I can't have messed you up any worse than I messed up myself. But we can put it right,' he said coaxingly. His lips slid over the smooth line of her forehead. 'Give me a chance to put it right,' he murmured, and at the same time his fingers traced a delicate pattern over the inner skin of her wrists as he lightly caught hold of her and drew her closer.

Jessamy gave a small shudder. During the short time their marriage had lasted, there had been so many times when she had given in to Julius's forceful demands, just to keep the peace. Now, for once, he wasn't demanding but asking. The habit of giving in to him was still hard to break, though, even after all the years they had been apart. Or perhaps there was a part of her that *wanted* to give in. That enjoyed being playfully submissive, because of the many delights she knew would follow.

He lifted one hand and slid it around the slim column of her neck. Then he stroked her lightly, soothingly, as if determined not to make any sudden movements that would startle her.

'Don't——' Jessamy muttered, but her voice was almost inaudible.

'I have to.' His breath fanned her skin as he leant towards her. 'You're the only one who can put things right for me.'

His hand moved from her neck and wandered down to the soft fullness of her body. Jessamy shivered, then shivered again as his fingertips rubbed lightly against the small hardening peaks beneath her T-shirt. Her body was already responding, although her mind was still stubbornly clinging to the last few threads of resistance.

Julius gave her another kiss, his tongue lightly probing, finding the well-remembered pleasure spots. And with the kiss came a sudden rush of memories; not of the arguments, the long silences, the hurtful remarks, but of the good times they had had together. There had been a lot of them, particularly in the beginning. They came back now, and she softened as they flitted through her mind. And with the softness came a dangerous vulnerability.

She recognised it, but couldn't seem to do anything

about it. Not while Julius's hands moved over her with quickening need, his skin burned steadily against hers, and his voice murmured in her ear, the words unintelligible but his tone telling her something she had never expected to hear again.

She shivered, then shivered again, but not from cold. Her skin was already beginning to radiate an answering heat, and the familiar flames started to lick along her nerve-ends. She found herself reaching out to touch him in return, closed her eyes and told herself to stop, but couldn't. Her fingers shook as they traced the familiar outline of chest and shoulders, strong back, flat stomach. It was as if she had needed to do this for such a long, long time, but had only just realised it.

He pushed her back gently on to the bed. 'Sorry there aren't silk sheets and satin pillows,' he murmured.

'I don't need them,' she said in a low voice.

Julius's eyes bored down into hers with a sudden hot light. 'Then what do you need, Jessamy?'

She swallowed very hard. 'I think—I think that I need you.'

She hadn't meant to say it, just as she had never meant to touch him. She couldn't seem to stop the words coming out, though. And Julius's breathing had altered radically almost before she had finished speaking.

His hands swept down and began to remove their clothes, first his own and then hers, and he had been right, his fingers did fumble a little, but she didn't mind that. In fact, she liked it; it made him seem more human.

As soon as her breasts were free of their thin cotton restraint, he licked the soft, warm flesh, as if the taste of her was something he had been craving for an eternity. Jessamy closed her eyes and wondered how she had lived without this sweet physical contact for so long. She realised that she had only been half alive for the last four years. She needed Julius to make her into a complete person.

She forgot about the coarse sheet that grazed her back. Instead she almost dreamily let her fingers trail over Julius's smooth and supple skin, she felt the hard heat of him against her palms, and it was astonishing how right it seemed that they should be together like this.

He touched her almost tentatively, and his hands were unsteady again now. He lifted his head and, in the semi-darkness, she could just make out the wry smile that touched the corners of his mouth.

'I'm nervous,' he admitted softly.

Jessamy stared up at him in amazement. *Nervous*? Julius was never nervous about anything!

'It's been such a long time, and I want you so much that I could easily make a mess of this,' he confessed.

'No, you won't,' she said equally softly.

His dark eyes bored down into her. 'Make it easier for me. Tell me you still love me.'

Jessamy almost stopped breathing. He was asking too much of her! There were some things that she just wasn't ready for yet.

'Tell me,' he ordered again, and bent his head and lightly nipped the soft skin of her breast. She didn't feel pain, only a small burst of pleasure that intensified as he then licked her reddened skin. 'I want to hear you say it, Jessamy.' His head dipped and his teeth nipped again, only this time at the vulnerable baby-soft flesh of her inner thighs.

Jessamy heard herself give a small gasp. 'Don't——'
she managed to get out before she choked into silence
again.

'Why not?' His tongue licked softly. 'You like it and
I like it,' he said, his voice muffled now as his head
became buried between her legs. Waves of heat washed
over her, and she felt his own skin burning against
hers. 'But I need to know that you like it because *I'm*
the one doing this to you. That you couldn't feel this
way with anyone else.'

'There's—there's never *been* anyone else.' She didn't
know how he had forced that admission out of her, she
only knew it was something she had to say.

Julius slid up to lie beside her again, and his eyes
were glittering very brightly. 'Not in all the four years?'

'I never wanted any other man.' It was the nearest
she could come to saying what he wanted her to say. It
seemed to satisfy him, though. But it also undermined
his already fragile self-control.

His mouth closed over hers and at the same time his
body abruptly demanded entry. Jessamy found herself
remembering how it had been the very first time
between them, it had been exactly the same, this
sudden *wanting*. She ached, she burned, and it was
Julius doing this to her; only Julius who could bring the
relief and pleasure that would release her from this
intense need. She craved the hardness of his body, but
it had to be him, there was no other man in the whole
wide world that she wanted.

The touch, the feel, the heat of him made her want
to laugh and cry. His mouth refused to release hers,
and every movement he made sent her spiralling
deeper into an apparently bottomless pit of pleasure, it
washed over her, saturated her, invaded every one of

her nerve-ends until she didn't think she could stand it any more. She said his name, the sound of it muffled against the pressure of his lips, and he murmured something back to her, moved with sudden fierceness, and the final thrust of his body sent them both tumbling down and down into a completely new dimension. She shuddered as convulsively as he did, and became lost in the same giant whirlpool of pleasure.

The intensity of it stupefied her. Even after it was finally over, faint echoes of it still quivering through her body, only fading very slowly away, she couldn't move.

Julius raised his head, although his body remained locked against hers, heat and sweat and shared pleasure fusing them together.

'Now will you tell me you still love me?' he said in a hoarse voice.

Jessamy briefly closed her eyes. It was impossible to lie to him. It was impossible to do anything except admit something that she had known for a very long time.

'I still love you,' she whispered.

And she wondered what that admission was eventually going to cost her.

CHAPTER NINE

JULIUS fell asleep soon after that. Jessamy knew he was perfectly relaxed, and his breathing was quiet and even. She certainly wasn't relaxed, though. For a long time she lay awake, staring into the darkness and telling herself that she had been absolutely crazy to let this happen. And even crazier to have told him that she loved him.

The only trouble was, it was the truth. For the last four years she had struggled to forget about him, to make a life for herself without him. Now she finally had to admit that it had all been a total failure. She was never going to forget Julius.

Confused and troubled, and with her body still gently glowing from the pleasure it had shared with the man lying next to her, Jessamy closed her eyes and tried to shut everything out. It was impossible, though. *Nothing* was ever going to wipe out the memory of tonight.

A long time later she finally drifted into sleep. She slept unexpectedly soundly, and when she next opened her eyes, daylight was filtering in through the rather grimy window.

She blinked, started to stretch, but then suddenly sat bolt upright as she remembered everything that had happened last night.

She discovered that Julius was sitting beside her. His hair was tousled and he still looked a little sleepy, but he was fully dressed, which made her feel at a distinct disadvantage.

Hurriedly Jessamy scrambled into her clothes. Then she ran her fingers through the long strands of her hair, getting rid of the worst of the tangles and flicking it back from her face.

'How long have you been awake?' she asked edgily.

'About half an hour.'

That meant he could have been sitting there, *looking* at her, for all that time. Jessamy definitely didn't like the idea of that.

'I think there are a couple of things we ought to get straight,' she said with some determination.

Julius's dark gaze rested on her calmly. 'What kind of things?'

'Last night——' She broke off because her voice had begun to quaver. She cleared her throat and tried again. 'Last night was a mistake,' she said very firmly.

'The only mistake we made was to wait for four years before trying to sort out our lives,' Julius replied in an unruffled tone.

'Last night didn't sort out anything at all!' she retorted.

'Of course it did.'

Jessamy shook her head a little desperately. 'Julius, you can't settle anything in bed. I thought that was a lesson we learnt a long time ago!'

'I'm not talking about the time we spent in bed. Although that was extremely pleasant, and something I'd like to repeat at the earliest possible opportunity,' he added, his eyes glinting brightly.

'Then what *are* you talking about?'

'I think you know very well. Or are you going to go on pretending that all we did last night was make love? That nothing more important happened?'

Jessamy could feel confusion sweeping over her. She

also knew it was very dangerous to feel confused when Julius was around. He was so very stubborn and single-minded when he went after something he wanted. She would need all her wits if she were to stand any chance of getting away from him.

The question was, of course, *did* she want to get away? Yesterday she had been absolutely determined that she did. Last night had completely undermined her resolve, though—as he had fully intended it should.

She went over to the window and stared out. She had to think this out very carefully, because the rest of her life was going to be affected by any decisions she made today. But she couldn't think straight while Julius was standing just a couple of feet away! She could feel the force of his personality even though she wasn't looking at him. It drowned out her ability to think clearly—in fact, her ability to think at all! She had to get away somewhere on her own, before she found herself blurting out things she had never meant to say, making decisions that were swayed by the influence he still had over her.

'I think I want to go back to the house for a while,' she said at last in a careful tone. 'On my own,' she added.

'I thought you didn't ever want to set foot in there again?' Julius reminded her.

'I'm not going to stay there. I just want to——'

'Get way from me?' he broke in, and there was a sudden edge to his voice.

She swung round and stared at him almost angrily. 'Look, don't try and push me into anything, Julius. Just for once, let me make my own decision. If you try and throw your weight around, force me into something I don't really want to do, then we're both going to regret it.'

The fierce glow slowly faded from his eyes. 'In other words, you don't want me to behave in my usual bull-headed manner.' He gave a dry smile. 'It's difficult, but I'll try. All right, go wherever you like and take as much time as you want. But make sure you make the right decision in the end, Jessamy.'

The throaty way he said her name made her knees gently shake. Afraid she might give in quickly and completely if she stayed here any longer, she made a dash for the door. Even when she was finally outside, in the morning sunshine, she had to fight the urge to turn round and rush straight back to that flat over the stables—back to Julius.

She forced herself to walk steadily towards the house. She didn't really have any idea why she was going there. It was just as good a place as any to get away from Julius for a while.

She pushed open the front door, which he had left unlocked. This wasn't London, and no one around here bothered too much about security. She walked through the large hall, her footsteps echoing off the stone-flagged floor, but then she suddenly stopped. What on earth was she doing here? She wasn't going to be able to reach any sensible decision while she was anywhere near this house. She needed to go back to London, to her own flat, where she could be sur-rounded by familiar possessions and be near to her family. Then she might—just might—be able to think straight.

She turned round and quickly began to walk back towards the door. There must be some way she could get away from here. Perhaps she could ring for a taxi, to take her to the nearest station?

Preoccupied with her own thoughts, and her mind still whirling with confusion from everything that had happened last night, Jessamy didn't hear the car draw up outside; didn't hear the front door open and then quietly close again. She had no idea she was no longer alone in the house until Eleanor walked into the hall, high heels clicking on the stone floor.

When she saw Jessamy, her cool green eyes became positively frosty.

'I didn't think you'd still be here,' she said shortly.

Jessamy slowly raised her head and faced the other woman. 'Why?' she said evenly. 'You didn't really think I'd run away just because you tore up a few of my clothes, did you?'

There was only the smallest flicker of reaction on Eleanor's beautiful face. 'Have you had some sort of accident with your clothes?' she enquired politely.

Jessamy suddenly grew tired of the silly games that everyone seemed to have been playing with her lately. 'I know you did it, Eleanor,' she said bluntly. 'Just as I know you sent that poison pen letter. What did you hope to achieve, though? I mean, what was the point of it all?'

There was an abrupt change in Eleanor's expression. The poised self-control seemed to disintegrate, and the green eyes began to glint a little wildly.

'What did I want to achieve?' she said tightly. 'I wanted to get rid of you, of course. Frighten you away, so that you'd never come back. You're no good for Julius, you never were. I knew it would be a complete disaster for him if you came back into his life.'

'And, of course, there was the fact that *you* wanted him.'

For a moment, Eleanor's gaze gleamed with triumph. 'For the last four years, I've had him!'

'No, you haven't,' Jessamy said steadily. 'You've been his secretary, and that's all. Anything else has been entirely in your imagination.'

'You're wrong about that!'

'No, she isn't,' said Julius's voice from the doorway.

Eleanor went completely white, and Jessamy gave a small sigh of relief. She didn't think she could have gone on handling this by herself, not on top of everything else that had happened.

Julius came further into the hall, and his face was set into very grim lines. 'I knew from the very start that you sent that poison pen letter, Eleanor. For my own reasons, I let you go ahead with your despicable plans. That was wrong of me, but it in no way mitigates your own actions. I should bring a criminal prosecution against you. A few months in gaol is the very least you deserve for what you've done.'

She stared at him in disbelief. 'But you can't do that to me. You need me!'

'I don't need you,' he said brutally. 'I've never needed you—except as an efficient secretary.'

Eleanor looked as if he had actually hit her, and for a few moments Jessamy found herself feeling sorry for her.

'You can't involve the police in this,' Jessamy said in a low voice to her husband.

He was silent for some time. 'No, I suppose not,' he said at last, although with great reluctance. 'A small part of the fault was mine for not noticing that Eleanor considered me as a great deal more than her employer. I was blind, and she was stupid.'

'She was in love,' Jessamy said quietly.

Her husband gently raised one dark eyebrow. 'And we both know that can make people behave in a very strange way,' he said drily. Then he turned back to his secretary. 'You need medical help, Eleanor,' he said more crisply. 'If you agree to my helping you in that direction, then we'll look at this situation again in a few weeks, when you'll hopefully be in a more stable state of mind.'

Eleanor's eyes had gone completely empty, as if Julius's blunt words had knocked every little bit of life out of her.

'I'll give you the address of a man I want you to go and see straight away,' Julius went on. 'I'll phone him, and let him know you're coming.' He looked into her blank face. 'Do you understand what I'm saying?'

She nodded very slowly. 'I'm—I'm——' Her voice was quite flat, with no sign of the bitterness that had edged it earlier, or the mad rage that must have possessed her when she had destroyed Jessamy's clothes. 'I'm sorry,' she finally managed to finish. 'I—don't know why I did what—what I did. It was like someone else doing it. I don't understand why I've done all these things.'

'I think you've had some kind of breakdown,' said Julius in a slightly gentler voice. 'The man I'm going to send you to see will help you to understand it, to cope with it and to get over it. Now wait here while I make a couple of calls.'

Although Jessamy still felt a little sorry for Eleanor, she didn't want to stay in the same room as her. She went back out into the bright sunshine while Julius made all the arrangements for Eleanor's departure.

Twenty minutes later a taxi arrived. Eleanor got into it, as quiet and malleable now as a puppet. The driver was given directions to take her to the doctor that Julius had contacted. Then she was driven away, out of their lives.

'Will she be all right?' asked Jessamy as the car disappeared from sight.

'The man I've sent her to is very good,' said Julius. 'I explained the problem to him, and he thinks he'll be able to help her.'

'Will he be able to cure her of being in love with you?'

'I don't suppose so. But I hope he'll be able to make her understand that she can't ever have me, and that she has to make a life for herself away from me.'

Jessamy gave an inaudible sigh. Poor Eleanor. She was about to find out just how difficult it was to live without Julius.

She began to walk very slowly back towards the house. Julius followed her, and stopped her as she reached the doorway.

'And what are *you* going to do now, Jessamy?' he asked in a voice that had suddenly become much more taut.

'I think I want to go back to my flat in London,' she said in a low tone. 'There really isn't any reason for me to stay here any longer.'

'Wasn't last night a good reason?' Julius said challengingly.

She rubbed her forehead tiredly. It was getting hard to think straight again.

'I'm beginning to think that last night was a mistake,' she muttered. 'It really shouldn't have happened.'

'But it did happen,' he reminded her, and there was a definite edge to his voice now.

She kept her gaze pinned to the ground, refusing to look into his dark eyes. 'Perhaps it would be better if we both tried to forget about it.'

'And are you going to forget that you told me you still loved me?'

'I can try,' she said defiantly. 'We made a mess of things once, Julius. I can't go through that same mess all over again.'

'Why shouldn't it be different this time?'

She struggled against the almost overwhelming urge to give into the hope that it could be different. In the end, she won. How could it be different? It would be exactly the same as before: they would be good in bed—at least, for a while—but hopeless at living with each other.

'Nothing's really changed,' she said, with a defeated shake of her head. 'I'm not the sort of wife you need, Julius. I never was, and I never will be. Your parents knew that the very first time they saw me. Socially unacceptable—that was your mother's verdict on me. And she was right.'

Anger glinted briefly in Julius's eyes. 'You wouldn't be living with my mother, you'd be living with me. And I don't want a perfect hostess. I never did. If I'd wanted that kind of wife, I'd have married Eleanor.'

'Perhaps you should have,' she said a little desperately.

'But I didn't want Eleanor,' he reminded her, his dark eyes beginning to glow. 'I wanted you.'

'But it didn't work between us! We couldn't talk. You *wouldn't* talk!'

'Haven't we talked these last few days?'

'Well—yes, I suppose so,' she admitted.

'Then why can't we keep on talking until we finally get through to each other?'

Suddenly she put her hands over her ears. 'I don't want to listen to any more of this!' she said fiercely. 'I've made up my mind, Julius. I'm going. I've *got* to go. And if you really do have any feelings left for me, then you won't try to stop me.'

She bolted through the open door, and all the time dreaded the touch of his hand on her shoulder, stopping her. Julius didn't move, though. Instead, his dark eyes just looked at her with a haunting intentness as she ran away from him.

Inside, she dashed towards the phone. 'A taxi,' she told herself shakily. 'I need a taxi.'

She lifted the receiver, then realised she didn't know what number to ring. And there didn't seem to be a phone book. An irrational panic started to set in. She began to feel she was never going to get away from this house; away from Julius.

As if saying his name to herself had magically conjured him up, Jessamy heard his voice behind her.

'If you like, I'll give you a lift to the nearest station.'

'I'd rather take a taxi,' she said in a stilted voice. 'I don't want to put you to any trouble.'

'Any trouble!' he echoed in a suddenly explosive tone. Then he seemed to get some sort of control over himself again. 'The phone will automatically dial the number of a local taxi firm. Just press the second button down.'

Jessamy lifted the receiver and went to press the

button. Then something else hit her. 'Oh, no!' she exclaimed. 'What day is it?'

'Sunday,' replied Julius.

She glanced at her watch, then groaned out loud. 'I should have been at my parents' house an hour ago! They're giving me a birthday party today. The whole family are coming, it's all been arranged for ages—and I'm not there!'

She forgot about the taxi, and instead hurriedly dialled her parents' number.

Her mother answered the phone. 'Hello?' she said in an anxious voice.

'Mum, it's me.'

'Jessamy!' exclaimed her mother, with a huge sigh of relief. 'We were getting so worried. Why aren't you here?'

Jessamy sighed. 'It's a very long story. I'm afraid I'm not going to make the party, though.'

'Why didn't you let us know?' said her mother rather reproachfully. 'We were beginning to think something had happened to you, especially when we kept ringing your flat and couldn't get any reply. Where on earth are you?'

'I'm——' She hesitated, then rushed on, 'I'm at Julius's house.'

'Oh,' said her mother, and somehow she managed to put a whole world of meaning into that one short syllable.

'Don't get the wrong idea,' Jessamy said quickly. 'I'm only here because—well, because there was a little bit of trouble.' That was a major understatement, but she didn't want to go into all the details right now, especially with Julius standing right beside her. 'It's over now, though,' she went on, 'so I'm going back to my flat. I'm really sorry about the party.'

'Never mind about the party,' said her mother. 'You're safe, and that's the important thing.'

Jessamy certainly didn't feel very safe, though. Not while she was still under Julius's roof.

'Perhaps you should stay with Julius for a little while longer?' suggested her mother hopefully. 'It's been such a long time since you've seen him. You must have a great deal to talk about.'

Jessamy gave an inward groan. Her mother had always adored Julius. Even after he had walked out, she couldn't bring herself to say anything unkind about him.

'I'm leaving as soon as I can get a taxi,' she told her mother very firmly.

'Are you sure that's the right thing to do?' said her mother persuasively. 'Why don't the two of you give yourselves some time together? You might be surprised at how things turn out.'

'I'm sure I'd be absolutely astonished,' said Jessamy, in a brittle voice.

'I read your stars on your birthday,' went on her mother. 'And they were very optimistic about all aspects of your love-life. I know you've had problems, but Taurus and Libra can be a very difficult relationship. It can also be spectacularly successful, though, if you work at it and get it right. Of course, Julius is *very* Taurean,' she added with a small sigh, 'but if you're clever enough—and love him enough—you should be able to handle him.'

'Put a ring through the nose of the bull and gently lead him?' Jessamy said drily.

'You certainly won't get anywhere by trying to be as

stubborn as he is. Anyway, I hope it works out for you. Give my love to Julius, and ring me some time next week to let me know how things are going.'

'OK, Mum,' she agreed, with a wry grimace. ''Bye for now.'

She put down the receiver, turned round, then felt her nerves give a hefty twitch as she found that Julius was still standing very close.

'My mother sends you her—her regards,' she muttered, for some reason not even wanting to say the word 'love'.

'I like your mother,' remarked Julius.

'And she's always liked you.' Jessamy gave a quick scowl. 'Most women like you.'

The darkness of his eyes became more pronounced. 'Including you?'

She decided she didn't want to answer that. Instead she picked up the receiver again. 'I'm going to ring for that taxi.'

Julius immediately took the receiver away from her and replaced it on the rest. 'No, you're not.'

She stared at him suspiciously. 'What do you mean?'

'I've decided you're not going anywhere.'

Jessamy's blue eyes began to flare. 'You can't stop me!'

'Of course I can,' he said in an unruffled tone. 'I'm bigger than you, stronger than you—and I've got another advantage, because I know that you don't actually want to leave here.'

'I certainly do!' she shot back at once. She was alarmed to hear a very obvious lack of conviction in her voice, though. Oh, if only she knew exactly what she *did* want! Usually she was very clear-minded. She hated being so confused, so uncertain.

'How long are you going to keep this up, Jessamy?' he enquired, looking at her now with new intensity.

'Keep what up?' she said warily.

'Pretending that everything's exactly the same as it was when you first came here. Pretending that you can go back to your old life, and forget all about these last few days.' His tone altered and became a little huskier. 'Pretending that you can live without me.'

'You're so arrogant!' she said with a sudden surge of nervous anger. 'Of course I can live without you. I've managed it for the last four years, haven't I?'

'No,' he said with some certainty. 'You've simply existed. That isn't at all the same thing as living.'

'How do you know what it's been like?' she accused.

'Because it's been exactly the same for me,' Julius said simply. 'Everything flat and grey, no real joy over anything, nothing to look forward to, just somehow getting through each day as it comes and giving a sigh of relief when it's finally over. That isn't living, Jessamy. And I don't want to go on like it for any longer. Nor, I think, do you.'

That stopped Jessamy saying anything for quite some time, because it was a frighteningly accurate description of how her life had been since their break-up.

'I've already told you we can't go back,' she said at last, in a subdued voice. 'At least, *I* can't go back. I mean it, Julius. I admit that life certainly isn't perfect at the moment, but at least I can cope with it. I couldn't cope with another break-up, though.'

'Then let's make sure we get it right this time,' he said softly.

'How can we do that?'

'We talk to each other. We give our relationship top priority over everything else. And we don't let anything—or anyone—interfere in our private lives. Not my parents or my work schedule. Not your career or your hard-won independence. We can't go back, Jessamy, but we can go forward—and on our own terms. You're more mature now, and I hope I've learned a few lessons from the mistakes *I* made. We can make it, if we really want to.'

Stubbornly she shook her head. 'I don't think I can do it. It all sounds too frightening.'

'What's frightening about it?'

'Everything!' she burst out. 'And especially you.'

Julius looked astonished. '*I* frighten you?'

'Of course you do. I was scared to death when I married you because I *knew* I wouldn't be able to be the kind of wife you needed. Your parents knew it, Eleanor knew it, and they were all proved right, weren't they? Then, when everything fell apart so quickly, that scared me even more, because failing at something like that is just about the most frightening thing that can happen to you.' The words kept on tumbling out of her and she couldn't seem to stop them. 'I don't think I'm any good at marriage, Julius, except perhaps in bed, and even that didn't last, it all went wrong. You see, I kept blaming you for everything, but that wasn't fair, a lot of it was my fault too, and I might make the same mistakes all over again, and I couldn't bear that. I hate hurting you, I hate it more than anything else in the world, but I *did* hurt you, and I'd sooner die than do it again.'

Julius caught hold of her shoulders and very lightly shook her. 'The only way you're going to hurt me is by running away from me,' he told her in a rough voice. 'And there's no need for you to be frightened of anything. We've both changed during the time we've spent apart. You're older, you've completely grown up, you can cope with anything and anyone—even me,' he added, with a wry twist of his mouth. 'And I've learnt that you have to open up and talk to someone if you want to get really close to them. All right, we're still going to have problems, but this time we're going to face up to them and deal with them—together. Jessamy, we can't spend the rest of our lives apart. Not unless we want to lead a grey, miserable, empty existence. So you don't think you can be a perfect wife? But I don't want perfection. I want *you*. And I don't want to change you, I want you exactly the way you are.'

Jessamy tried to put up one last feeble show of resistance. 'I still think you'd be much better off with someone like Eleanor,' she said in a small voice.

'Forget about Eleanor,' he ordered. 'She isn't important, never was important—except that she gave me a chance to get close to you again.'

'Your parents won't like it if we get back together.'

'My mother will probably have a very genteel fit of hysteria, and my father will mutter something about it being a "damn shame" and your not being "the right kind of girl", and then stomp off for a game of golf. They'll eventually get used to the idea, though,' he said equably.

'I suppose I could try and make them like me,' Jessamy said doubtfully. 'Perhaps I could learn how to give dinner parties. And I could occasionally wear a dress instead of paint-stained jeans.'

'I told you, I don't want you to change in any way,' Julius said more huskily. 'Either they like you the way you are, or not at all. Whichever they decide, it isn't important. *I* like you. In fact, I love you. And nothing else is very important, is it?'

Jessamy was finally beginning to believe he was right about that. And he was right about something else as well. She didn't want to leave here. In fact, she didn't want to go anywhere unless he came with her.

She couldn't quite believe she was taking the first few tentative steps back towards her marriage. It was so dangerous, she warned herself rather breathlessly. But, quite suddenly, she liked the feeling of danger, the small tingle that ran through her nerve-ends, the goosepimples dancing lightly over her skin. After all the grey years, she was beginning to feel marvellously alive again, and she suddenly laughed out loud.

'This is crazy!'

'Of course it is,' agreed Julius. He bent his head and kissed her. 'Just how crazy do you think we ought to get?' he asked softly.

'I don't know.' He kissed her again, and she felt her head begin to spin. And the first small tongues of flame ignited somewhere inside her.

Julius's hands slid underneath her T-shirt, his palms as hot as her own skin. As the kiss went on and on, he pulled her closer and closer until she could feel every warm, hard inch of him imprinted against her.

A few moments later he raised his head, to catch a gasp of breath and then to mutter softly in her ear, 'There hasn't been a day—or night—in the last four years when I haven't missed you. Wanted you.'

'I suppose we ought to be grateful to Eleanor,' she said wryly. 'She set out to drive us apart, and instead she seems to have brought us together.' Then she caught her breath lightly as Julius's fingers delved into the soft warmth of her body. 'Do you think we ought to be doing this?' she said in a rather strangled voice.

'Why not?' he murmured. 'We're still married. We can do absolutely anything we like.' And, while she was still digesting that piece of information, he added, 'And I can think of dozens of things I'd like to do, beginning with a kiss and ending——' He broke off and gave a faint grin. 'Perhaps I'll let the ending come as a surprise.' Then his face became more serious and his dark eyes fixed on hers with a new intensity. 'But first I want to promise you a couple of things. The first is that I'll never walk out on you again. And the second is we're going to have a very different kind of marriage this time. One that works, and one that lasts.' Julius kept looking directly into her own blue eyes. 'Do you believe me?' His gaze became much more intense. 'It's very important that you believe me.'

'Yes, I believe you,' Jessamy said softly. And it was the truth. They were older, wiser; they had learned many bitter lessons. They would be more careful with each other this time because they knew how easily human beings could be broken and hurt.

He visibly relaxed again. 'Good. And now all the serious things are out of the way, it's time for a little fun.'

'Fun?' echoed Jessamy.

His fingers slid down again and lightly tickled her, provoking small, exquisite sensations. 'First I'm going to make you laugh. Then I'm going to make you cry. And then I'm going to make you say my name in a way that you've never said it before,' he told her huskily.

Jessamy buried her face against her husband's shoulder. She still couldn't quite believe any of this was really happening, but she had the feeling that Julius was about to *make* her believe it—and in the most delightful way possible.

During the last few days she had been sent a poison pen letter, had her life turned upside down, and now she was in the arms of the man whom she had been absolutely determined to divorce. It had been a very strange week!

Then Julius's mouth closed over hers again, his hands began a series of loving, teasing caresses, and Jessamy forgot everything except that this was her brilliant, stubborn, bullish husband whom she loved very much, and a bright future suddenly shone in front of them.

STARGAZING

YOUR STAR SIGN: **TAURUS (April 21–May 21)**

Taurus is the second sign of the Zodiac, ruled by the planet Venus and controlled by the element of Earth. These make you obstinate, purposeful, reliable and—sometimes—rather self-righteous. Your high degree of motivation, endurance and need for security makes you carry out plans thoroughly with resolute attention to details—up to the point of stubbornness!

Socially, Taureans are known for their motto: 'Eat, drink and be merry'—you possess an earthy sense of humour and have a pragmatic approach to life in general. As the second and most fertile sign in the Zodiac, building a secure and comfortable home is your main concern and every effort is directed towards that goal.

Your characteristics in love: Charming and dependable, Taureans tend to be incurable romantics and enjoy giving presents to their loved ones. They are loyal when it comes to relationships but like to take things at snail's pace to be extra sure of sweethearts before committing themselves. Nevertheless, once you are in love, you are an extremely faithful partner to the extent of being possessive and see red once the bull in you is unleashed. You prefer to choose marriage rather than living together with your ideal partner since it helps boost your craving for security.

Signs which are compatible with you: **Capricorn**, **Virgo**, **Cancer** and **Pisces** are the most harmonious, while **Gemini**, **Sagittarius** and **Aquarius** provide you with a challenge. Partners born under other signs can be compatible, depending on which planets reside in their Houses of Personality and Romance.

What is your star-career? Taurean philosophy is to take root and then grow when it comes to career matters. Once an appropriate career is found, such as music, industry, building, landscape gardening and accountancy, you will work with steadfast enthusiasm and develop skills without being confronted by any sudden changes.

Your colours and birthstones: Taureans have a good sense of colour and feel soothed by the colour of the sky: pale blue and pink, but never red—as any bull fighter will tell you.

Your birthstones are diamonds and emeralds; both stones enhance the practical femininity of a Taurean as well as being a good investment. Diamonds are the purest tokens of love, while the emerald has a tradition of healing eye diseases. Even today, some believe that tired eyes can be revived with water in which an emerald has been soaked overnight.

TAURUS ASTRO-FACTFILE

Day of the week: Friday
Countries: USSR, Ireland and Cyprus
Flowers: Violet and poppy
Food: Oysters and Dover sole; Taureans are great food-lovers and have acute tastebuds but—being creatures of habit—they will stick with their favourite recipes.
Health: Although you have a sturdy constitution, take care not to over-indulge in the good life—or you might regret it later on in life! Watch your weight and treat yourself to sensual therapies such as body massage and saunas.

You share your star sign with these famous names:

Perry Como   Cher
Michael Palin   Queen Elizabeth II
Lloyd Honeyghan   Maureen Lipman
Peter Howitt   Audrey Hepburn
Pope John Paul II   Selina Scott

Accept 4 Free Romances and 2 Free gifts

•FROM READER SERVICE•

An irresistible invitation from Mills & Boon Reader Service. Please accept our offer of 4 free Romances, a CUDDLY TEDDY and a special MYSTERY GIFT... Then, if you choose, go on to enjoy 6 captivating Romances every month for just £1.60 each, postage and packing free. Plus our FREE newsletter with author news, competitions and much more.

**Send the coupon below to:
Reader Service, FREEPOST, PO Box 236, Croydon, Surrey CR9 9EL.**

✂- - - - - - - - - - - NO STAMP REQUIRED - - - - - - - - - - -

Yes! Please rush me my 4 Free Romances and 2 Free Gifts! Please also reserve me a Reader Service Subscription. If I decide to subscribe, I can look forward to receiving 6 new Romances every month for just £9.60, postage and packing is free. If I choose not to subscribe I shall write to you within 10 days - I can keep the books and gifts whatever I decide. I can cancel or suspend my subscription at any time. I am over 18 years of age.

Name Mrs/Miss/Ms/Mr _____ EP17R

Address _____

_____

Postcode _____ Signature _____

Mills & Boon

Next month's Romances

Each month, you can choose from a world of variety in romance with Mills & Boon. These are the new titles to look out for next month.

THE GOLDEN MASK ROBYN DONALD

THE PERFECT SOLUTION CATHERINE GEORGE

A DATE WITH DESTINY MIRANDA LEE

THE JILTED BRIDEGROOM CAROLE MORTIMER

SPIRIT OF LOVE EMMA GOLDRICK

LEFT IN TRUST KAY THORPE

UNCHAIN MY HEART STEPHANIE HOWARD

RELUCTANT HOSTAGE MARGARET MAYO

TWO-TIMING LOVE KATE PROCTOR

NATURALLY LOVING CATHERINE SPENCER

THE DEVIL YOU KNOW HELEN BROOKS

WHISPERING VINES ELIZABETH DUKE

DENIAL OF LOVE SHIRLEY KEMP

PASSING STRANGERS MARGARET CALLAGHAN

TAME A PROUD HEART JENETH MURREY

STARSIGN

GEMINI GIRL LIZA GOODMAN

Available from Boots, Martins, John Menzies, W.H. Smith, most supermarkets and other paperback stockists.

Also available from Mills & Boon Reader Service, P.O. Box 236, Thornton Road, Croydon, Surrey CR9 3RU.